Steffan Gilbert

Stories From The Hollow

AF205022

Steffan Gilbert

Stories From The Hollow

Southern Gothic on Wry

JustFiction Edition

Impressum/Imprint (nur für Deutschland/only for Germany)
Bibliografische Information der Deutschen Nationalbibliothek: Die Deutsche Nationalbibliothek verzeichnet diese Publikation in der Deutschen Nationalbibliografie; detaillierte bibliografische Daten sind im Internet über http://dnb.d-nb.de abrufbar.
Alle in diesem Buch genannten Marken und Produktnamen unterliegen warenzeichen-, marken- oder patentrechtlichem Schutz bzw. sind Warenzeichen oder eingetragene Warenzeichen der jeweiligen Inhaber. Die Wiedergabe von Marken, Produktnamen, Gebrauchsnamen, Handelsnamen, Warenbezeichnungen u.s.w. in diesem Werk berechtigt auch ohne besondere Kennzeichnung nicht zu der Annahme, dass solche Namen im Sinne der Warenzeichen- und Markenschutzgesetzgebung als frei zu betrachten wären und daher von jedermann benutzt werden dürften.

Coverbild: www.ingimage.com

Verlag: JustFiction! Edition ist ein Imprint der
LAP LAMBERT Academic Publishing GmbH & Co. KG
Heinrich-Böcking-Str. 6-8, 66121 Saarbrücken, Deutschland
Telefon +49 681 37 20 310, Telefax +49 681 37 20 310-9
Email: info@justfiction-edition.com

Herstellung in Deutschland:
Schaltungsdienst Lange o.H.G., Berlin
Books on Demand GmbH, Norderstedt
Reha GmbH, Saarbrücken
Amazon Distribution GmbH, Leipzig
ISBN: 978-3-8454-4564-9

Imprint (only for USA, GB)
Bibliographic information published by the Deutsche Nationalbibliothek: The Deutsche Nationalbibliothek lists this publication in the Deutsche Nationalbibliografie; detailed bibliographic data are available in the Internet at http://dnb.d-nb.de.
Any brand names and product names mentioned in this book are subject to trademark, brand or patent protection and are trademarks or registered trademarks of their respective holders. The use of brand names, product names, common names, trade names, product descriptions etc. even without a particular marking in this works is in no way to be construed to mean that such names may be regarded as unrestricted in respect of trademark and brand protection legislation and could thus be used by anyone.

Cover image: www.ingimage.com

Publisher: JustFiction! Edition
is an imprint of the publishing house
LAP LAMBERT Academic Publishing GmbH & Co. KG
Heinrich-Böcking-Str. 6-8, 66121 Saarbrücken, Germany
Phone +49 681 37 20 310, Fax +49 681 37 20 310-9
Email: info@justfiction-edition.com

Printed in the U.S.A.
Printed in the U.K. by (see last page)
ISBN: 978-3-8454-4564-9

Table of Contents:

Dedicated

To my beloved kith and family, who helped me learn to love language's delights;

To my trusty bubs and karmic kin, for the fun we have orienting notions to fruition's sights;

To my beloved Constance, for helping me see the ways in which toget it right

And in the name of all light, may peace be upon you and yours upon this night.

A Delivered Sign

The good Pastor Sidney Daniel Huddleston arrived in Defeated with his family on a beautiful late summer day and went to heaven in a wheelbarrow from there.

The drive from Memphis seemed to last twice as long as it should have, and for once not because of the never-ending unspoken contention between Beverly and Erin and himself. The distraction was a gorgeous morning.

The potted asphalt gleamed from storms the night before. Clouds reflected the dawn into a soft salmon haze that permeated the landscape. Moving east from the flat lands and flood plains of the state toward the central highlands, the hills and trees played tag with the shadows cast by sun over clouds.

When they passed the state highway sign welcoming them to Nottamun County, Beverly scanned the roadmap.

"We're almost there." As she listened to her voice she was caught off guard by how eager she spoke.

As they came closer to Defeated, the number and breadth of lakes rose, until they merged into one long shoreline of cedars and water and sky.

The car curved through the end of a seventy-foot stretch of limestone and they passed an elegantly sturdy log home.

Beverly pointed to the front yard where a wild turkey wandered, casually alert, looking for breakfast. There was a white cat in the yard as well, a dozen yards from the unapproachable bird. The cat had just given birth, her teats still full as they braced the side of her body. Poised to leap, she stared in wide-eyed awe as she considered this epic hunting opportunity. Beverly laughed hard at the notion of a cat that would stand up to such a formidable challenge. She had to roll down the window to get air, and during the rest of the ride would attempt to bring it up every twenty minutes or so, only to stutter back into silence from laughing.

For the first time in many years, he felt like they were a family again. Beverly was warm and open, even affectionate toward her husband and daughter. Erin seemed finally content with her lot in life, in which having to spend her senior year at a new high school was equated with inexorable, psyche-scarring abuse. For the last three weeks, Erin had been engaging in breath defying oral and blogged manifestations of Gothic suicidal daydreams.

They passed and noted a neat green metal sign with white lettering, welcoming them to Defeated. It was not so much a city as it was a rural afterthought. A general store and a gas station gave the only indication of any urban activity at all.

As they approached a compact white picket square of a building, a couple in their early sixties standing at the road waved their car into a paved cul-de-sac large enough for a score of vehicles.

The church deacon and his wife, who followed them into the empty parking lot and patiently waited while the Pastor parked the car with near painful precision, greeted them. Mr. Dixon was dressed in a clean white shirt and pressed pair of carpenter overalls. His baseball cap had seen a rich life, however, and carried motes of dried muck from hundreds of fishing spots. His missus, dressed for the warmth of the day, was comfortable in a Hawaiian muumuu. They each carried a covered dish. Their rustic appearance dismayed the fashion sense of Huddleston's wife and daughter, while simultaneously enhancing the feeling of moral superiority within the Pastor.

"I'm Dow Dixon and this here is my wife Daisy', said the portly man, gesturing to his portlier wife. "We wanna thank you and the Good Lord for comin' so soon in response to our letter. We brought y'uns some peach cobbler and poke sallet. My wife's recipes. She's done won first place at the poke sallet festival in Gainesboro three years running now."

"Poke sallet?"

Erin was dubious. For the first time in many a year, the three Huddlestons were in perfect simpatico with each other.

Driven by uncharacteristic curiosity, Beverly waved a brown bang from her neat plucked eyebrow and looked quizzically at the clear blue casserole dish.

"What on earth is poke sallet?"

Daisy Dixon smiled broadly at Beverly, who was in turn trying not to stare rudely at Daisy's crooked front teeth or the missing ones at the left side of her mouth.

"Little sister, are y'all in for some good eating! First you gather up a bucket or two of poke leaves, only you have to get 'em young 'cuz they turn all poison on you once it gets too late in the year. You boil 'em twice, to steam out the bite and toughness, then you fry 'em up in bacon grease and eggs. You never tasted anything else as good, I tell you that."

The Pastor looked back to see his wife and daughter gaping like fish in a boat. He glared at them quickly and they shut their mouths. No use in alienating these people now, and he surely didn't want things to end up like they did in Memphis. After all, he told himself, it wasn't *his* fault that the congregation lost faith in him; it was the poor attitude of his wife and daughter. He did love his wife and child like lambs in the flock, but sometimes he almost felt they were more trouble than they were worth.

"Thank you for your consideration, Mrs. Dixon. I'm sure we'll find it a very . . . filling dish for dinner tonight. Now, if we could get to the church?"

The Dixons looked at each other and laughed. It was not a malicious laugh. The Huddlestons were not used to hearing *good*-natured laughing at their expense. The Pastor felt his skin flush and the old bile begin to back up in his throat. Beverly and Erin, used to the warning signs, stepped back and turned to the side, to keep them out of harms way. They also felt a bit safer having witnesses there. It had saved them in Memphis.

The Dixons nodded their heads in unison toward the plain blockhouse behind them. The building the Pastor had assumed was the community center, or perhaps a warehouse.

"Won't have far to go, Pastor. Not much to look at, but she fairly rings with Sunday morning and Wednesday night hymns. Don't feel embarrassed – you don't need to get all awkward and red faced – you among friends here. Truth be told, most folks miss it unless they know it. Unless you see the church signs yonder on the grass there."

Dow's attempt at being comforting was successful enough that Huddleston lost some steam and Beverly and Erin relaxed a bit. Huddleston walked around to examine the signs. They were each on separate posts.

The higher wooden sign proclaimed this "The First Church of the Forgiven Redeemer'. The wood burned sign had seen many seasons and was still being lovingly cared for by the deacon. Huddleston was impressed by the craftwork on the sign. It was a rare event to impress the Pastor.

The sign next to it sat about six and a half feet tall, braced upon two metal posts set in concrete. The display unit was the type that could be back lit at night and kept the foot tall black lettering attached within plastic straps that went from side to side. The side facing him read *"Message on the other side"*

He turned back to Dow to question the choice of phrase. Dow shrugged with good nature, though he was also a man who felt he had more important things to attend to in his spiritual agenda.

"Well, you know over time weather and wear and tear happens, and we ended up with more letters for the other side. This side we just glued the letters to the sign."

Huddleston strolled a few feet along the road, and then glanced at the other side of the sign. In silence he read, lips moving, the message again. His face began displaying tell tale signs of rage once more. Dow noticed this and walked around to read the sign, on which the phrase had been changed to read *'Prepare to meet thy doG'*. A sheepish grin on Dow's part tried to mollify Huddleston's growing anger.

"Kids, you know,' Dow said apologetically. 'They get bored because there's so little to do on weekends."

"Aside from church, you mean." Huddleston made no attempt to hide his disdain for the lack of moral supervision he was now convinced permeated this area. Dow made it clear he could hear as well as the next man and was quick to speak for kith and kin.

"We have good people live here, Pastor. Just give them some time and you'll see we're all God's children."

"I'm sure." The Pastor replied, his voice dripping with at least two of the seven deadly sins.

For the next three weeks, the Pastor focused his sermons on the need to obey and honor and respect authority. Specifically, he entreated the self-imposed captive audience to respect his word of authority as an emissary of the Lord.

His intonations fell on at least one deaf ear.

During that time he had put up at least three different phrases on the church's outside display board, and each one of them had been altered.

"If they obey and serve him, they shall spend their days in prosperity, and their years in pleasures." had been turned into *"Anybody free, amidst hells hyphen, alien Sidney airdrops panty peruser hysteria thieves"*. This statement caused a number of befuddled parishioners to approach him courteously, asking for the book and verse that particular inspirational statement had come from, and what exactly it meant. A few

wondered why the Pastor was mentioned by name. This embarrassed Huddleston, who did not want his good name and budding reputation besmirched by a connection with ladies lingerie.

During the sermon the Pastor, unused to the tactic, tried to make light of the sign. He had his best response when he admitted in a cautious tone that he didn't know how to take the manner in which the sign had changed. Someone sitting in the pews spoke up, a reed thin young man with a self-propelled mop of unruly black hair atop his head.

"It's the Book of Sidney, Verse one – one."

The lanky churchgoer apparently didn't realize his words would carry that well. His family and friends held their hands over their mouth to keep in the spontaneous belly laugh, or slapped him on the back in a small quiet chorus of 'That's a good'un.' A bit self-conscious, he avoided the Pastor's glacial stare, which seemed to target him with laser precision throughout the rest of the sermon.

After service, many parishioners, shamed and mortified, came up to him and vowed that the sign would not be bothered again. They carried humiliation with a disquiet responsibility. Huddleston liked that in his parishioners. He changed the message that afternoon back to its original inspirational thought.

True to the word of the good people of Defeated, the sign was not altered again that week.

That next Sunday, he thought he had the answer. He awoke just after dawn and set the sign with the phrase *"Endure God's Wrath"*. He had timed how long it took to put the message up, assuming it would take at least that much time to change it again. He finished by seven and went in the house to get ready for the service.

Shortly after eight, the service was opened. As was his directive, Beverly and Erin came in before anyone else.

Some folks milled in yawning behind exhausted knuckles while a few other hearty souls braved a full body stretch. There was a fair amount of giggling from the younger ladies gathered at the foot of the stairs. When they saw Erin, they waved her over to them and whispered to her, their hands fluttering in the air. She stifled a squeal that was just milliseconds from erupting and went back outside quickly. The other ladies flew to their pew seats avoiding curious glares.

A few minutes later, Erin returned, her hands shielding her reddening face from the rest of the parishioners. She sat down next to the young women who were unsuccessfully trying to hold back giggles seething between them with the tempo of a pulse.

Huddleston came in, oblivious to the alteration, approached the altar, and began setting out books. The Dixons entered, sweating out their obvious discomfort. Dow watchfully approached the Pastor and whispered in his ear. Huddleston froze in mid motion.

Erin watched her father as stifled his choking rage, safe in the knowledge that she was too far away to be singled out. When he met her gaze, she stopped breathing for a second. He could hear her even when she was thinking, she feared. Resolutely, she concentrated on the sign, reddened and fought back her own laugh.

Huddleston strode purposely down the aisle, ignoring the swell of titillation that followed him. He drew in a sharp breath as he stepped briskly onto the walk, bearing down upon the sign like a pilot in a dogfight. He walked around to face down the display sign.

"Endure God's Wrath" had been changed into *"Andrew hugest rod"*.

"God loves an honest man and woman", he began his sermon that week, straying from his previously scheduled exegesis on why wrath was good.

"What God doesn't love is when some misguided sinner decides to insult God's house. This morning I had put up a message that I thought would be a worthwhile thought to consider until next week. And it was mocked. I do not want the people of this God-". Huddleston stopped rather than say "God-forsaken".

" -This God-fearing community to think that I would single them out for retribution. What God Almighty works through my hands is another matter. ."

He paused to scan the congregation, most of whom were rather perplexed and a few, mainly children, who were alarmed beyond their years. As the flock milled out after service, only a sure-footed few stared the Pastor eye to eye as they shook hands upon departing.

"Interestin' service" held consensus as the most frequent response.

Most disturbing to Huddleston was the changed message the third week, when *"Eternal Damnation awaits all sinners"* became *"Altar animations wanted an Erin sells"*. He was sure it was a slander against his virginal daughter.

It was not right for his family to be made targets. They were not strong enough. They weren't like him. He had seen to that as he ran his family into the ground.

Huddleston had learned throughout his life to carry a thick skin. Even as a child, his pasty pocked face inspired ridicule and his screaming fear of life defined his social interactions. The taunts had only made him impervious to emotional response. At Seminary, he concluded finally that the sin and temptation he saw around him at Seminary were just excuses to have God and deride him too. He would rise above his lessers at the Seminary, his adversaries in life, and he would show them all what benefits piety brought with its presence.

It despaired him that Beverly and Erin were not as strong. Beverly he could almost understand; she had always been a bit too malleable. He had hoped that Erin might catch his fire without being scorched by his willfulness. She was a private girl, though, who held to herself since elusive childhood. He tried thinking through things. He had never been very good at it, but he tried for the sake of the sanctity of his family. How could he protect his family? By the time Morning Prayer service started, he thought he had his answer.

The service that morning consisted of the fervent archetypal meat and potatoes laundry list of moral indignities and perilous lifestyle choices. His roll call for those vices was so inclusive that it condemned anyone who was in earshot, and the mouse in their pocket, to eternal damnation.

He was in such rare evangelical form that damn near every soul in the congregation avoided him on the way out. Grandmothers with no children and single folk with no prospects went out through the Sunday school door while those that could snuck out through the fire exit.

Huddleston didn't care about the escaping lemmings; he was looking for Zeb Miller, who ran the scrap metal yard and who was unanimously recommended as the best metal worker in the area. Huddleston waited by Zeb's truck as he approached.

"'Nother interestin' bit o'preaching, back there, Pastor . . .."

Zeb, a lanky, good natured man with a long sandstone colored braid that shouted defiance to his gray beard, spoke to Huddleston with a bit of caution, unsure what he might be asked to obligate himself to. Zeb didn't mind obligating himself as long as he had some say in the matter. Where the church was concerned, his experience was that they expected to have that say instead of him. And it was easier getting beer from a bee than pay from a church.

He waited for Huddleston to speak up, not appreciating that Huddleston was not familiar with the action of politely asking others for favors. Zeb rocked on his heels and watched the sky while Huddleston groped for the right words.

"Beautiful morning, ain't it?"

"What? Yes . . . why, yes – it *is* a gorgeous sky. . "

Zeb was consternated to see how unaware the Pastor was of his immediate surroundings.

Huddleston was genuinely startled by the sky, by the migration across the horizon of majestic white and graying cumulus canyons, by the shadows engraved into the billows. A jangle from Zeb's keys as he adjusted them in his hand brought Huddleston somewhat reluctantly back to earth.

"Zeb – I don't want to inconvenience you-"

'Here it comes.'

"I'm looking for someone to raise the display sign, so it - so it can be seen by more folks."

'Like Aunt Claire wants to show off Uncle Gill's pecker', thought Zeb, though he didn't say that.

"Church gonna pay for it?"

"Some. I'll make up the difference out of my own pocket."

"How high? You mean like one of those billboard signs?"

"Not that high, but with a little platform around it. Maybe twelve feet high."

"With scaffolding to hold up a man."

"Just me." replied the Pastor, before he realized what he'd said.

"Me and my son'll do'er for you Pastor. We'll have 'er up before your next service."

"Your son?"

"Junior. AJ. He wuz the one made that joke 'bout the Book of Sidney couple of weeks back."

"I see."

"Look, here's what we'll do yuh. I'll take 10% off the bill since he was rude that day. He can work free to pay it off."

Huddleston decided that was acceptable and shook hands on the deal. He then asked the fateful question.

"Your son was named for you?"

"Named for me, yes'ir."

"But your name is Zeb."

"M'people, friends call me Zeb. It's m'middle name. Zebediah. Andrew Zebediah Studds is m'full name. He's Andrew Studds, Jr."

'*Andrew hugest rod*', thought Pastor Huddleston.

Naturally, the work took nearly a month of Saturdays. AJ was in school during the week and the road commissioner hired Zeb to shore up metal work on the county bridges, and as most of them were over lakes, it became impossible to commit to any other job during the week. The Pastor watched from his house across the road from the church, marking the progress the sign was making. It soon became unequivocal to Huddleston that the two men knew what they were doing as they set about their business with impeccable professionalism. It was unusually hot for that time of autumn, so Zeb and AJ both worked in tank top tee shirts, which accented the excellent shape both men were in.

Beverly and Erin both seemed to dote on the father and son with lemonade and lunch as the men erected two twelve foot metal poles, atop which anchored the sign and then placed a catwalk around it so the sign could be changed. Huddleston never paid much attention to the men, busy as he was on preparing the Sunday service.

At the end of the final day of work, Zeb and AJ were invited to supper, which Huddleston vaguely protested. The supper was well received, the hostesses were charming, and the host was desperate to end the evening. Even after they left, as the women were busy in the kitchen, the chatter and stifled giggles suggesting the continued presence of Zeb and AJ.

During service, he could not help but notice the quick glances and subtle smiles exchanged between his women and the Studds.

After the service, as the three of them stood in the doorway, Zeb and AJ approached Beverly and Erin. Huddleston felt like an afterthought. Not that they didn't shake his hand and thank him for a sin biting sermon, which they did.

A couple of nights later Beverly told him that AJ was coming over after dinner to study.

It wasn't the short notice that caught in the craw of Pastor Huddleston; it was the way his wife and daughter fixed themselves up as if they were going out to Sunday dinner. It was only after he answered the doorbell that he understood what 'after dinner' meant. Zeb and AJ were joining then for dinner.

The Huddleston women both pressed the fact of how few good meals the widower and his son probably had, and did so with such rare determination that for once the Pastor threw up his hands. He would not dare debase his purity by giving in to craven jealousy. Only righteous anger was pure, and Huddleston was full of that.

It was Tuesday night and before dinner plates were in the wash, the Pastor was busy putting together his Wednesday night sermon and lettering the sign. While Zeb and AJ were being offered their choice of desserts, Huddleston was twelve feet in the air.

"Where there are no righteous, the sermon is always dry."

After a final nod of satisfaction for his inspirational message, Huddleston climbed down a small metal ladder at the east side of the catwalk.

Huddleston opened a recessed panel inside the left post, which had been cut out by Zeb, then replaced the ladder within the cranny. He glanced around to make sure he was unobserved.

It was almost unheard of for a church message to be changed in the middle of the week. It just wasn't done. Huddleston could hear them even now in his mind, he supposed, their caw-caw patois beleaguering him.

He suddenly didn't care about the petty concerns of his pedestrian flock. About the fast pitched, good-natured conversational tones he could hear through the closed windows of his own house. He *WAS* God's chosen shepherd. Above all, he held to that abstraction.

The Wednesday night congregation, which was not as crowded as usual, found Huddleston's sermon to be less accusatory while more patronizing. Huddleston used silhouettes of a silken voice to promote his version of the nuclear family. That it might be God's version as well was an afterthought at best.

There was little interaction between Huddleston and the assembly as they left. They were all too tired. Upon the last worshipper departing, Huddleston went back in and straightened up the pews. It was later when he left the church later that night that he noticed the sign.

"Don't you realize what they're doing to you behind your back?"

There was no way. How could anyone change the sign that quickly? Someone had dared to defile a tool of the Lord. As an officer of God, it was up to him to rectify the matter. That night, he changed the sign once more, to read *"Those that challenge the righteous shall perish from the Earth"*.

That would show the town where he stood.

The next morning he awoke to find the sign now declaiming *"Even if you knew how you were being betrayed, you'd be too weak to change"*.

Zeb and Dow went all the way to Faye's Café in Gainesboro to talk about the problem with the Pastor. Daisy joined them and so did Harvey Seadon, who was the mayor of Defeated. He listened, unconvinced, to Dow's defense of the Pastor.

"I ain't sayin' I'm a disagreein' with yuh, Harv; I just think he'll get out of this mind he's got his'self into right now."

Dow was conciliatory toward the question of what to do with Huddleston; he knew what a pain it was to install another new pastor without having given this one a chance to work out. Harv was having none of it. Leaning back in his chair in the fluid motion that always signaled his intent to hold the floor, he smoothed back his dark wavy hair with both hands then slid his thumbs in a tight arc into his suspender straps.

"I tell you fellers; that man is one teacup short of a picnic lunch. He gets me so sour after one of his sermons that I can't hardly eat a thing without it come back on me the rest of the day or night. He's got Betty so nervous I have to purt' near pull her out of bed on Sundays. Then come Wednesday she's always got something in the oven or on the stove. And she's not the only one starting to be too busy to show up at church. I know Daisy's been talkin' to Betty and I bet most other wives in town. Isn't that right Daisy?"

Daisy, ignoring the debate by design, was quietly talking truck parts with Zeb.

"I just wanted to check. You still got the rear gates, right, Zeb?"

"Y'bet."

"Daisy, don't change the subject. You ain't never been one to hold back your opinion before; why clam up now?"

Daisy and Dow, who had gone to high school with Harvey, knew how well he liked to bait folks into a brawl. Dow also knew his wife could hold her own with anyone during a squabble.

Daisy had been staring at her lap during Harvey's interrogation, hoping to blend into the background. She smoothed her skirt slowly and with purpose unknown. When she spoke, it was in a tone of voice so restrained that the men moved closer to hear her.

"The simple fact is we need to respect the Pastor. We aren't ever going to know God's ways just by what his messengers ask of us. Or of him. We don't know how God is testing him. We can only let his trial be our trial, as it was with Jesus. We'll be delivered a sign. Let our faith in that work its way through, please, Harv?"

"I've done that for weeks now, Daisy. And where is he right now? I bet he's just standin' on that damn sign, puttin' up some other doom and gloom message just so he can say one of the folks in the pews went and changed it. I'm getting' tired of this, I tell yuh. I say show his sorry ass the door and let Dow preach 'till we find a replacement."

Zeb observed Dow's unenthusiastic shifting in his seat and decided to add his two cents.

"The man's as friendly as an Osage Orange tree. Can't deny that. Guess, though, if you hire on that school of preachin', you'd best expect a little bile with the fire and brimstone. As long as he ain't hurting his family or the community, don't see no harm in him stayin' here 'bouts. I'm with Dow."

Harv knew Zeb well enough to know his decisiveness. Nevertheless, he opened his mouth as if preparing a response, which moved Zeb to talk to Daisy to close off discussion.

"I guess you'll be drivin' m'truck 'till I bring yours back, Daisy."

Huddleston stood in front of the damned sign and examined his latest doom and gloom pronouncement.

"Woe will be unto them who dare defileth the work of my Lord's hand!"

It had occurred to him that he was not thinking clearly these last few days; perhaps, he thought, he was being prepared for an epiphany. After all, he reasoned, who needed secular logic in the face of the Lord's over powering will?

He went inside to calm his nerves with a cup of chamomile tea. After some fifteen or so minutes, he went back outside to see if the forces of darkness were again meddling with his ministry. Oddly, he thought, he was almost elated to see the sign changed; it was something he was starting to depend on.

"You're being played for an idiot and you'd better do something about it right now!"

The sign was right, he realized with a shudder.

Beverly and Erin had gone to Nashville to shop and see the sights and when they got home; if they got home, he thought, if they didn't just go straight over to Zeb and AJ's house and share their day and their bodies with them . . .

The mental picture of his wife undressing, her auburn hair wet on Zeb's pillow, his daughter's lighter hair sweeping gently over the face of AJ, mingling her hair with his, her fluids with his, drove Huddleston into new paroxysms of impotent anger. He went into the kitchen and grabbed the bottle of French brandy they used for fancy dinners. Just a sip to calm my nerves, he thought. Just a sip.

By the time he had finished what was nearly a full bottle, he thought he had his plan.

On unsteady legs he made his way out to the sign and brought out the ladder. It took a half-hour to finish the new message.

"Damnation! I will smite who takes what is mine!"

On the way down he lost his footing and slid the last few feet back to the base. As he landed, he heard an engine and turned to see Zeb's truck idling a few yards ahead of him, then continue down the road. Huddleston smiled a tight dangerous grin. He had a new plan. The car. No, Beverly and Erin had the car. He ran to the church van. The keys were in the ignition because this was a community where you could trust folks. After a few minutes of trying to turn the engine over, he started up the van and pulled into the road. He pushed the van to sixty miles an hour in an attempt to catch up with the two home wreckers. All he wanted to do was to talk with them, that was all. Tell them not to fornicate with his wife and daughter; that was all.

It took only a few minutes on the now dark winding road to catch up with the truck. The van moved closer. Just a nudge was Huddleston's plan. He bumped the back of the truck. The truck picked up speed.

'*Oh no*', thought the capricious and good Pastor, '*you won't evade my wrath that easily.*'

He bumped the truck again as they were approaching a bend in the road. This time the truck's brake lights lit up. They were going to stop.

'*Good for them*', thought Huddleston as he stepped on the gas pedal.

He hit the truck harder than he thought he would and watched with detached satisfaction as the truck went over the embankment and down the side.

He pulled up to the shoulder and rolled down the window, listening to the truck crashing through the underbrush. After a few moments, he heard only the soft whirring of the truck's engine as he watched his breath fog in the cold air.

'*Now, I guess I can offer Samaritan services.*'

He got out of the van, trying to maintain balance as he walked to the edge and looked over the side of the embankment.

The truck had landed on its roof, crushing the occupants, who were both hanging halfway out of the shattered windows.

The headlights bounced off the trees in front of the truck, softly illuminating the immediate darkness around the broken bodies of Dow and Daisy.

Huddleston blinked and rubbed his eyes. It was Zeb and AJ, he told himself at first. He stood for another few seconds, getting his bearings and clearing his mind. No amount of mental clarity would change the fact that he had killed the church deacon and his wife.

With a searing sob that tore itself from the Pastor's throat he flung himself away from the accident scene and made his way back into the van.

"*How did this happen?*" he asked himself, as if he had been an innocent bystander.

Suddenly, with vicious precision, he understood. It was the sign all along.

That damned sign had led him to doubt his family, his flock. That damned sign had led him from the arms of his Lord. He couldn't bring Dow and his wife back, but by God, he could make sure that damned sign didn't lead anyone else astray.

As he drove back to the church, his anger and anguish fought each other for prominence. As he approached the church, he slowed the van to a crawl, so that the sign would be unaware of his presence.

He knew now what he had to do.

He put the van in park and began revving the engine. He put the van in drive and roared toward the sign, hitting it on the right side. The post buckled.

He backed up a few feet and hit the post again. The sign stayed up, refusing his personal crusade to fall.

He put the van in reverse and prepared to do battle once more. This time he aimed the van, now hissing steam and moving crookedly on its front wheels, toward the left post and slammed into it.

Huddleston leaned slightly out of the driver's window when he heard the creaking metal. He was just in time to see the corner of the heavy sign fall toward him. Not enough time even for a prayer of penance.

When Beverly and Erin came home an hour or so later, they were met by the volunteer fire department and by Zeb and AJ, who explained the loss they and the community had to deal with. Beverly wanted to see the damage. The entire front of the van had been crushed by the impact of the display sign, and the last message Pastor Huddleston would put up was still, amazingly, intact. Beverly, Erin, Zeb, and AJ read it.

"A man cannot buy his way into righteousness, no matter what price he may pay"

It took another two months for a new Pastor to be brought to the community. Zeb, who had been asked to be the new deacon and reluctantly agreed, met him at the church with Harvey in tow. The new Pastor's name was John Melia, a fresh scrubbed man of innocence who had just finished his training at the Bible College.

"We think you'll like it here, Pastor", Harvey said. "Nice town, good folks. 'Ceptin' for that tragedy a couple months back. It's all settled now, though. The church was left money from the last deacon, and the whole town decided to replace the church sign with somethin' modern, one of them there LDD-"

"LCD – Liquid Crystal Display." Zeb gently corrected Harvey

"Right – one of them kind of signs. Ummm – you ain't got no problems with that kind of sign, the modern ones, do you, Pastor?"

Pastor Melia smiled and shook his head. Harvey was clearly relieved to hear this.

"Well, that's great, just great. Best thing about this kind of sign is that you can change it from inside the church. Stay warm and dry that way. Figured we'd wait and turn it on to welcome you."

Harv walked over to the post and flicked the power switch on. A smattering of letters crossed the front of the sign as it warmed up and then settled into the welcome for the new Pastor.

"Prepare to meet thy doG", it read.

Elvis Has Expounded The Building

The kids always look so cute when they play alien invasion, putting up their Fisher-Price defense shields around their friends. You can look out over the neighborhood any nice day and see rows of domed shells dotting the lawns like antique pink flamingos. These precious lumps of cherubs are so involved that most do not hear the plaintive, sometimes nasal entreaties to come in for lunch or dinner or bath time. Moreover, not one of them, almost certainly, heard the two top items of the news downloads that particular day.

The first item was about the crash of a van and a hearse. A sealed coffin, whose occupant was not heard to complain, and the driver, who was examined on the scene and released, occupied the hearse. The hearse was also unaffected, though suffered some structural damage. The van, however, carried a dozen patients from a nearby clinic, where they were being treated for Kornheiser's Syndrome, and each of the passengers suffered a variety of contusions and abrasions.

Owing to of their viral infection, most didn't even remember what it was like to be involved in a vehicle crash and most certainly wouldn't recall the crash within forty-eight hours.

Medical science had another term that clarified their physiological condition: Lucky Bastards.

The other item of interest was more like a theological 'Where Are They Now?' It concerned the disappearance of the corpse of the late twentieth century icon known as Elvis Presley from his shrine in Graceland. Much plaintive wailing was to be heard from his adepts, who were evenly divided between those who cursed the vanishing and those who were certain it was the beginning of the Resurrection of Saint El the OTB {Omniscient Teddy Bear}. Already the net broadcasts were beseeching the teeming multitudes that worshipped on line at the church to make sure their tithe cards were current and their accounts in order.

Of course, those who saw a sinister conspiracy believed that there was more to this than met the eye. They saw the theft, if it was such, as a blatant attempt to undermine the Prophecies of Jesse.

These canons, channeled through an ancient Elvis Head lamp, prescribed that if His sanctified remains were to abide in the hands of the adepts, they must be preserved in a scaled tomb at any cost. The methods of removing His Holy Hipness could range from common theft (which the adepts considered unlikely, given the tight security at Graceland), to the ascribed though never verified 'Miracle of Mother Gladys'. Once his artifacts left the hands of the faithful, they would, in the words of the canons, "Be not seen by any but the blissfully ignorant, uh-huh." This inspired the Catechists of the church to suggest that any cost incurred could be paid as a monthly charge off the believer's credit chips. Much more plaintive wailing was heard from the spouses and life partners of those in the church, who acutely felt the pinch of their loved, one's economic martyrdom.

Tim had left Julia due to her devotion to the church, having decided that the price of divorce was far cheaper in the end than the investment in Saint El's deification. He had his locksmith livelihood to provide barter and income, even though he was not a trained locksmith as one might find the job defined by anyone not easily distracted by shiny objects.

That is to say, he was not trained in the electronic systems that secured most entryways in this day and age. He preferred the old fashioned methods, like pure force. He might have thought of himself as a Luddite, except that he rarely exercised that portion of his anatomy involved in the cognitive process.

Tim had been contacted earlier that morning to open a locked door at 546 Fenway. Contacted so early, that in fact, he was still waking up when he took the call. He would be the first to state he was not to blame if he had been given the wrong address.

He parked in front of 654 Fenway. Tim looked around; expecting to find the homeowner waiting for him, as he had been told would be the case. Cheez, he thought, some people can't even be bothered to be on time to their own emergency. He walked around the house, thinking the residents were in the back yard. No such luck. He crossed back to the front of the house, looking along the street. He went back into his vehicle.

Distracted, he opened his auto net link and listened to the news about the disappearance while he considered his options. He looked at the time. It was getting late and he had a birthday party to get to yet. His friend George, the rich old weasel, could always be counted on throw quite the bash. He ticked off the to do list in his head. Break in; then dash over to the bazaar to pick up a gift for George, and get to the party before the food was stale and the women all gone.

He looked again at the time, tapping his fingers on the steering wheel. To hell with it, he decided. The owner probably went to the store. Would be right back. Yeah, he was sure they'd be right back. In the meantime, he'd open the door and that way he'd be ready to go as soon as they returned and paid him.

He got back out and walked around the house again, this time looking for some point of access. The windows weren't any help. They were all too high to reach without a ladder of some sort. Besides which, Tim was afraid of heights. There was a back door, but Tim decided he didn't need the hassle of some security drone pepper spraying him, or worse, juking him with some taser blast. Nope, he thought, it's the good old front door for me. Easy in, quick and clean.

The front door, however, was as solid as a rock. The entry pad wasn't going to help him out, either, even if by some miracle he could figure out how to fix it. It was one of those fiber optic gizmos tripped by the eyeprint of the owner. Tim looked at the pad quizzically. Why would they need me to open a locked door if all they need is their own two baby blues? He shrugged. They weren't paying him to be a problem solver. He was being paid to open doors, and open them he would. Maestro, the crowbar.

He set at his job with gusto, easing the bar into the doorjamb, sensing for the weak spot. This door isn't built like most, Tim thought. After a few minutes of ineffectual jabbing, it occurred to him that stronger measures were required.

He spit on his hands, because his dad had spat when there was hard work to be done, as had his dad before him and his dad before that. The women in his family always checked twice before holding anybody's hand. Out came the sledgehammer. The first 'thud' was very loud, and not effective at all in opening the door. Tim squinted in disbelief and examined the door. Only the slightest dent was observed.

'Must be stiff this morning', he concluded, and gave the door another good whack. The dent grew imperceptibly; as did the realization that the door was reinforced in some way.   After tapping the door a few times with his knuckles, Tim became convinced that there was a metal plate behind the door.

"Now what fool would do that?" He asked aloud. He rubbed the dent, which was a bit more pronounced that he had realized with his fingers. No wonder they need me to open this door, he contemplated.   'Puter sensor must be malfunctioning.

He went back to his work with what could be considered surgical precision, if you consider Jack the Ripper a surgeon. He believed the door was starting to give way when he noticed the hearse approaching from over the hill.

He knew from hard experience that it was better to let a vehicle pass rather than incur the pointed looks and sometimes raised weapons that sometimes accompanied these occurrences. To his dismay, the hearse slowed as it neared him. The vehicle stopped as it passed Tim, then backed up into the driveway of the house where Tim was working.

Tim felt the same flush of contrasting emotions that came upon him whenever a homeowner came upon him as he toiled. The mixture of feeling relieved at the owner finding him working and feeling dismay at the owner finding him attacking his front door. The observation that a hearse was involved did not bring cool ease to Tim's brow, for some reason.

The driver got out of the hearse. He was preternaturally tall, over six feet six inches, and equipped with a hologarb emitter, which was set to mimic the traditional somber work suit of a mortician. Unfortunately it was malfunctioning, because the faux Hawaiian Shirt and Bermuda shorts he was wearing underneath were clearly visible as the unit phased in and out. Tim noticed that the bumper and rear door of his hearse was severely dented. The rear window had crone's fingertips of crannies rippling up from the bottom of the glass.

Through that window, Tim saw the coffin. From where he stood, it looked like there was masking tape around the coffin going from top to bottom. The hearse driver unlocked the door to the house next door and entered, paying Tim no mind whatsoever as he closed the front door behind him.

Tim looked at the house next door and gave the door he was trying to open one more solid blow with the sledgehammer. Tim's heart wasn't in it, however, as obsessive curiosity seeded within his mind. Who was in that coffin anyway? Tim knew that he could clear a lot of rewarding bankstrips if the hearse contained Saint El. And if not, well - he just didn't think that far ahead.

He set the sledgehammer on the ground, leaning its handle against the doorknob. He visually canvassed the streets quickly then moved toward the hearse. He peered into the rear window and saw it was not tape but twine that was binding the coffin. In the window's reflection Tim's sandy, curly hair seemed to be even more disheveled than usual, and his lean face, with its high cheekbones, appeared to him to be even slightly longer. He considered how he might open the hearse's rear door.

Meanwhile, the labor that Tim had put into opening the door he started out with was starting to pay off. Slowly, silently, the door began to part. Tim was busy cupping his hands over the window, trying to see if there was a latch he could utilize. The door swung open about a foot and stopped. The door's movement was caught by a pair of feet, which belonged to a male body lying prone on the floor. The body was restful, unmoving. He was apparently a young man, wearing an antique black leather ensemble. His hair was done up in a mid twentieth century hairstyle known as a 'duck tail', and was slick black. There was a sneer on his lips, which made him seem even more menacing.

Tim, at the back of the hearse, saw none of this, though he heard the door of the house the mortician entered opening and tried to jump away from the vehicle before he was spotted. His gaze met that of the mortician, who let a brief frown cross his face.

Tim turned away, trying to be nonchalant and let his eyes wander around the yard and finally back to the door he had opened, whereupon he saw the body on the floor. The mortician was moving toward Tim too quickly for Tim to get to the front door and close it before the mortician met him. Unsure if the body was there as a result of his slamming the door he decided to keep its existence to himself for the time being. As the mortician approached him, he met him at the hearse and positioned himself so that the mortician would be less likely to see the body through the doorway. The mortician walked toward him unhurriedly, giving the hearse only a cursory glance.

"Howdy." The mortician was affable. "You look a little too healthy to be interested in taking this ride."

Tim laughed; hoping it didn't sound too forced.

"Not me. I - umm – was just curious as to who your – ahh – passenger was."

"Well, suppose I could show you. Don't think he'll get too riled up about it."

Tim blinked. He couldn't easily turn down the offer, and he had some prurient interest in seeing what a dead body looked like. Still, he didn't want this guy to see the body in the doorway. He might want to compare notes.

"Well – that's a tempting offer, but I'm on the clock here."

As soon as Tim said the words, he regretted them. If he was on the clock, what then was he doing peeping in a hearse? "Just was finishing my lunch and now I have to get back to work."

He said this slowly, as if emphasis on each word would add to their truthfulness.

"Oh yeah? What is it you do?" The mortician seemed truly interested in his vocation.

"I'm a locksmith. I'm working on the house here, trying to get in for the owners."

"Hah – ain't that something? Here I thought you were one of the owners all along. Worried me for a second you might object to me leaving the hearse in your driveway. I keep such odd hours that I never seen 'em. Say - maybe you could show me a few smithy tricks."

The mortician started to turn toward the house. Tim did the only thing that he could think of doing.

"You know, come to think about it, I am awfully interested in seeing your . . . rider. You mind if I have myself a look?"

The mortician turned to face him and seemed quite pleased that someone was showing curiosity in his profession. He beamed a broad smile and set about opening the back of the hearse.

"Had me a little accident this morning. Some dag-nabbed van not paying attention in the fog ran right into me. Good thing Junior back there wasn't in a complainin' mood. The folks in the van were okay, I guess. Didn't hear them complain. They got that Kornheiser's thing. Gave them something to forget, I bet."

The mortician guffawed nasally, and Tim smiled politely, hoping to get this thing over with.

As jauntily as one can with sullen skin, a gaunt complexion, and an intermittent Hawaiian shirt can, Mr. Undertaker moved to the back of the rig, took off the twine sealing the casket. He lifted the lid enough so that Tim could see the corpse within, who was dressed in a white cowboy suit.

Tim had never seen a real cowboy suit, as it was much easier to hologarb one's self in whatever attire one desired.

"Those are real clothes?" Tim asked, somewhat incredulously.

"You betcha they are. Heirlooms, I heard.   Think it's the first time I ever buried anyone like this.   You wanna touch them?"

Tim was tempted, though decided against it. Even though he might not have another chance to run his hands over a real cowboy suit made of something more tangible than paper or designated electrons. He had his own carcass to think about. He wanted to check on whoever it was and get to George's birthday, hopefully without getting arrested.

"Well, I'd like to, I really would; but I wouldn't want you to get in any trouble. I'm sure there's places he's got to be."

The mortician closed the casket and climbed out from the hearse. He looked disappointed.

"If you say so. Most folks would pay a weeks worth of bankstrips to have this chance, though if you'd rather not . . .."

The mortician let his voice trail off, as if expecting a self-serving protest, or at the least a reconsideration. When none was forthcoming, he got in the driver's seat, started the hearse up, and slowly pulled out of the driveway.

Tim returned to the body inside the door. There was a slight odor once he leaned over the body. It was a slightly musty smell, reminiscent of formaldehyde. In Tim's mind, this alerted him to the fact that this guy probably didn't get this way on his account.

Tim also became aware of a nagging voice in his head that told him this was Saint El. Tim, who was still stumped as to what to get George, had a revelation as to the perfect gift, what to give the man who has everything: his own saint.

Quickly, Tim threw the body over his shoulder and carried him to the van. The body was surprisingly supple, not at all stiff, and Tim got him in without any problems and even better, without any witnesses. He briefly considered letting him ride in the passenger seat, then decided against it. He didn't need some zealous police officer thinking the sneer was meant as an insult. He sat him on the floor of the van behind the driver's seat, where he fit quite snugly. Tim sat the sledgehammer on the Saint's lap to hold him in place, and his sneer seemed even more justified because of this action.

He started the vehicle and set off, feeling not only work efficient but downright gleeful as well. As he passed a house a few blocks away, the couple standing in front began waving their arms and trying to chase after him.

'They'll just have to find another locksmith', Tim thought. *'I'm going to a party. Funny coincidence, though, their address being 546 Fenway'*.

When Tim arrived at the party, he was grateful it was still going in full swing. Nothing he liked less than a party that was winding up as he got there. He looked around for George and saw him standing in the middle of a group of people. As he approached the group, he could hear George's resonant voice.

"So she asked me why I'd want to go to Long Beach for a vacation. I told her: 'the same reason some people go to Key West – it was there and I was here."

Everyone laughed heartily at this; most everyone tended to enjoy George's talents as a raconteur. He stood a solid six feet, with curly black hair and blazing blue eyes. Despite, or perhaps because of, his wealth, he had a wide variety of friends and acquaintances, from a disparate group of humanity. George had one arm around Lowe, a News Imager George had known for years, and the other arm around his mother's shoulder.

Mae was a vibrant woman, still very youthful at seventy. Rumors abounded as the source of her vim and vigor. Most gossip had the echo of envy about it, attributing her good looks to chemical or surgical means. George maintained that it was just 'good genes'. Considering George himself looked near thirty though was nearer forty-five, no one questioned it, at least in front of George or Mae.

She was currently black and white, having undergone the latest in trendy fashion accessories; a treatment that, when complete, made the wearer look as if they had stepped out from one of the halftone films from the previous century. When done well, as it had been where George's mother was concerned, the effect was startling at first glance. She was dressed in a stunning outfit that Tim was almost certain was real clothing; after all, she could afford the best.   Mae wore a long dark torso dress and was adorned with a rope of pearls that stretched from her neck to her navel. Her still dark hair was in a high bun, a pompadour, Tim heard her refer to it as to another guest who was fawning over and complimenting her.

Tim paid his respects to the birthday boy and to the humans draped under his arms, kissing Mae's hand. Tim stared for a long moment at the contrast between his hand, tinged in skin pigmentation, and Mae's hand, which was a starkly, stately gray.

Mae smiled warmly at Tim, pleased by his manners and George seemed genuinely pleased that Tim could make it, which only confirmed to Tim that he had done the right thing in his choice of a present.

"You'll never guess what your present is."

"My own sledgehammer?' George was a bit in the bag, and enjoying it.

" A new hologarber." Lowe piped in, though Tim would rather he hadn't.

Tim gestured for George to approach him. George disengaged himself from Lowe and his mom and leaned over to hear Tim.

"I brought you your own Saint."

George looked quizzically at Tim. Behind them Lowe was approaching. Being naturally nosy, and in the news gathering business, Lowe had developed his instincts to a fine hone.

"I ran across something I knew you didn't have, and I brought it with me." Tim was trying to be coy. As far as George was concerned, he was just being irritating.

"Tim, I can't imagine what it is."

Tim appeared somewhat crestfallen, as he had hoped to make a longer party game out of this.

"I didn't give you enough clues, is that it?"

"Tim, you haven't given me *any* clues. Just tell me what you got me."

"I found Saint El. He's in the van."

Lowe, who overheard Tim's comment, immediately began to look around to see if anyone else had heard Tim's statement. Tim noticed Lowe slyly pull out his imager, his predatory news instincts coming to the forefront. This Tim expected from Lowe. On the other hand, George's response was not what Tim expected.

"Are you insane? Do you know how many different security forces are looking for Saint El? What are trying to do – put me in a institution for the rest of my life?"

Lowe heard this, as did most of those assembled, and slid his imager back into a pocket.

"Well, why don't you have a look at him before you decide." Tim offered, trying to be helpful.

By now, the other guests were paying more attention to George and Tim's conversation than to their own interpersonal interactions. Mae positioned herself between George and Tim, looping their arms within each of her elbows. The guests began to causally meander off one by one to search for the location of Saint El.

"Darling, let's not make a fuss here. Your guests don't want their wonderful time spoiled, after all."

"And I don't want my wonderful time spoiled by Soldiers of El swarming in and grabbing me for conspiracy."

"I'm sure no one would do that."

"Mom, you don't understand. Saint –"

Mae drew herself up sharply and addressed her favorite only child.

"*I* don't understand? I give regularly to the Church of Elvology. I think I have a unique understanding of the dynamics here. What I don't understand is how I raised a son with such poor manners that he's unwilling to show a little appreciation to a dear friend who's gone to a lot of trouble for a one of a kind present." She glared at George, who did not back down.

"You're not the one who'd be sent to Indoctrination Camp. You're not the one who'd forfeit his holdings to the Church. Tim, I like you, even though you're a little absent-minded, but this is beyond the pale. Maybe I should turn you over to the El Guard. How would you like that, huh?"

Tim was crestfallen. He had never been threatened by George before, and certainly not with incarceration. He looked around to see if anyone had heard his dressing down. He was relieved to observe that only Claude, whom he had never liked much anyway, was near enough to pay attention.

Claude, who as usual was standing all by himself, felt particularly sorry for Tim as George was berating him. He knew all too sharply, what it was like to have people yell a lot. He thought of himself as the token screw-up, and those that knew him, or knew of him, would have agreed with that assessment.

He stood by the large pile of George's birthday gifts, prepared to tell anyone who asked what he was doing there that he was guarding the pile. After all, he reasoned, there were a lot of very expensive presents there, and anyone could walk into the party and walk off with any one of them; the bioneural 'puter, for example, or the 'Band in a Can' or even the molecular vaporizer, a very popular gift for the holidays. He turned his attention to George, whose voice was rising in irritability, glad that for once, he was not the focus of someone's anger.

"Tim, I am not gonna even look at it – what were you thinking in bringing Saint El here in your van in the first place?"

The guests, who had given up their search and returned to stand near George, began murmuring among themselves, then with those around them, building a cacophony of question and confirmation that culminated in a consensus to go to Tim's vehicle to see the Saint for themselves.

To get to the van, they had to pass Claude, who was noticeably nervous at the crush of humanity approaching. He picked up the vaporizer, not really intending to use it, just to brandish it so that the mob would find another route to go to get to Tim's vehicle. Flourishing the weapon had no effect on the crowd, who was following the ancient adage of straight lines being the shortest routes between two points. Without realizing it, his finger played along the triggering mechanism.

As the swarm of people came nearer, George tried to head them off to allow Tim the chance to leave and take the corpse back wherever he had found it. In the process, the crowd ended up carrying him on the curl of their movement straight into Claude. Not expecting the physical contact, Claude accidentally triggered the vaporizer, hitting George, who was slowly sandblasted into infinity, looking very perturbed at Claude as he vanished out of sight.

Now the partygoers had something new to be upset about. Growing cries of "What have you done?" and "Bring George back!" began to spread among the guests like a storm wind. Mae, seeing her son dematerialize, ran over to Claude, with Lowe just ahead of her.

Lowe, who had given the vaporizer to George and had read the directions, took the vaporizer from Claude's trembling hands. Resetting the device to 'Rematerialize', he triggered the vaporizer.

While he was setting the device, he had pointed the vaporizer a good dozen feet in the air, which is where George rematerialized, and since he was not wearing a zero gravity pack, he fell hard to the ground. The crowd as one yelled "Huzzah!"

Mae, who was horrified to see George's lovely party atmosphere disintegrate, along with her son, rushed to his side and began cooing over him as George picked himself up, slowly and somewhat painfully, though none the worse for wear. Lowe turned off the vaporizer, turned to Claude, and spoke very seriously indeed to him.

"Never pick up the vaporizer again."

Claude, who was still numbed by his faux pas, was not listening.

"W-What?

Lowe slapped him upside the head.

"Never pick up the vaporizer again. What did I say?"

"Never pick up the vaporizer." Claude replied glumly.

Lowe raised his eyebrows in disappointment and gave Claude's skull one more melon thump. Claude nodded, either in understanding or the onset of concussion and repeated himself.

"Never pick up the vaporizer *again*."

Claude spoke the last word very slowly to make sure he got it right.

Lowe ruffled Claude's hair as if he were a favorite pet.

"Very good."

The other partygoers, upset with Claude for nearly spoiling the festivities, each lined up to castigate Claude and reinforce the instructions not to pick up the vaporizer ever again. At the end of the line was George himself, who really wanted Claude to internalize the message, and so whacked him with particular emphasis.

George then turned his attention back to Tim, who was not sure if he would receive the next thump down.

"Tim, you can't leave Saint El here. I appreciate the thought, but I have no inclination to put up with the problems his presence raises."

Tim thought very hard.

"I can't take him back where I found him. I don't want to leave him by the side of the road."

Lowe approached George and whispered in his ear. Mae, who was still with George, listened in. Their muttering voices could be heard, and occasionally part of the discussion made it out of their huddle.

"Why don't we . . ."

"We already have the grand .

"Yes, but what a wonderful . . ."

"And it would get it off your . . ."

For the first time since George had been told about his gift, he smiled broadly and nodded. He motioned over two burly helpers, hired to help during the party entertainment, and whispered in their ears as well. They grunted and left, headed in the general direction of Tim's vehicle. George turned to Tim.

"Since it's my gift, are you saying I can do whatever I want with him?"

"Use him as a hat rack for all I care. Just as long as you get some use from him."

George turned and addressed the group.

"Friends, as you know, every year, as the high point for my birthday bash, I host a reenactment of one of my favorite forms of nostalgic entertainment."

The crowd, who had been waiting for this, signaled their approval by whooping it up.

"I'm ready to start it if you are!"

Again, the guests ranted in approbation.

"Alright, then, let's all go into the auditorium!"

The party moved into a large auditorium and sat patiently. George disappeared from view behind the curtain. The lights over the audience faded. The sound of the stage curtain opening could be heard. Suddenly the left and center of the stage was awash in light. On the left of the stage were three podiums, with a traditional LED indicator on each one. In the center of the stage, on the floor, was a large, round cavity which was in darkness, and one the side of the stage opposite the podiums were a number of items which were in shadows and could not be clearly made out. George's voice came over speakers placed around the auditorium.

"Missy, come on down!"

Missy, a very attractive woman in her twenties, bounced down the aisle and up the stairs to the stage, where she continued bouncing and squealing in delight behind one of the podiums.

George also called Lowe and Claude to the stage. Lowe mounted the stage with much panache, while Claude clasped his hands over his head in joyous victory at having been forgiven by George. Again, George's voice boomed over the audience.

"It's time to play . . ."

With one voice, the audience yelled out.

"*Wheel - - of - - Fortune!*"

The lights went up on the rest of the stage. The objects hidden in shadow turned out to be a late twentieth century washer and dryer, along with other household appliances more suited to a museum than a house. George, now dressed in a business suit, bounded out on stage and stood by the cavity. The light that illuminated him also lit up the wheel recessed into the cavity on the floor.

"Our contestants each have the chance to win these fabulous prizes, and one lucky person will take home our grand prize!"

With the loud joyful sound of the contest buzzer the games commenced, and to everyone's surprise, at the end of the contest, Elvis left the building with the one person no one would have ever expected to win such a prize.

George continued to throw wonderful parties, though he would never match that unusual birthday ever again. As time went on, he appreciated increasingly the gift Tim had presented him, and when Mae finally passed through the veil, he had her preserved after the fashion of Saint El, giving her a special place of respect in his foyer. He made it a point to invite Tim to every one of his birthday parties, where they would reminisce about Mae and wonder what ever happened to Claude.

After leaving the party, Claude was never seen again. As his unfortunate luck would have it, shortly after he arrived at his home, Claude contracted Kornheiser's Syndrome, forgetting even where he had acquired the nattily dressed stuffed mannequin wearing a sneer on his lips.

No one ever realized that Saint El was in the little bungalow that Claude called home. The neighborhood children, playful as ever, erected a series of defense domes around Claude's house, and left them there, where they keep would be onlookers away. So here Saint El rests, comfortably, to this day, protected by Fisher-Price.

The Way Of The Willow

Once upon a time, before you or I or even our oldest friends were born, this land, this very spot where we are now sitting warm and cozy, was a wild and fierce place. Then it changed.

Some say the change came through a mystic from the eastern seas, while others claim this organic alchemy was caused by a priestess from the rough dolmens to the northwest, who saw how much this place needed calm and so planted an oak.

Now; how much can an oak do, you say? I will say that this was no ordinary seedling, but one which had seen the first dawn, so long ago. Truly, the oak did slow so slightly that frenetic pace of that place and age.

The oak, though, was not alone in that tempest. Close by was a willow, ever so ancient, who decided to help the seedling, for that was the willow's way.

So the two of them, oak seedling and bending willow, watched time weave her quilt upon the land.

From the rocks, brooks, and then minute forests of lichen crept slowly forward, uncertain at first, though after a while bubbling with relaxed certainty. The rock gave way to soil. Through gales of rain and sheets of ice the trees stood, taking it all in concert.

At last, the sun shone through the murky gray. It was a remarkable sight. Everything from one horizon to the next was green and flourishing. This was a happy time for the trees, stretching their limbs and branches as far as they could reach, shaking their leaves and laughing for the sun. Moreover, the oak grew, until finally its roots intertwined with those of the willows. Ah, they frolicked. Yes - trees can frolic quite merrily without a twig of help from us, thank you very much; and they shared sights and sounds that only have meaning to trees, and some that only make sense to the wisest ones.

For us, time is a road from one side to the other. For trees, time rises to the skies. When the oak felt very far above the ground, the willow began to change for the worse. Its branches no longer grew as many new leaves with the season's change, and its boughs grew heavier with each passing storm. One morning, as the oak stretched and shook good morning to the season, it became as clear as crystal what was occurring.

The willow was preparing to elapse, to imbue yet another form with everything the oak had come to count on, sight, spirit, and soul. This trembled the oak down to the roots.

The willow stirred, and, sensing the concern of the oak, whispered through its branches;

"Soon, someday soon, ' The willow's branches rustled ever so slightly, "I will wind my way through the loam and on to new suns and breezes, and you will not follow me for quite a long while, though you will remember me by the birds that alight upon your boughs and the winds that whisper my memories. And one day you will share yourself with the light of all things."

They waited for the night together In the morning, as the first lark sang a welcome to the willow, the oak knew the willow had passed through to new loam.

At first, it was painful every morning for the oak, as the willow stood its ground. Nevertheless, slowly, slowly, the willow dropped bark and branch, providing for the earth's many small and smaller. Many found a home in the decaying trunk. The oak was rather put off by this, thinking it all together too rude a treatment for such a good friend; though that soon gave way to happiness that so many were able to make a home. One thing gnawed away at the oak's heart through all this:

"Is there not a tree with whom I can teach as the willow taught me?"

This thought gnawed at his heart over many seasons, though so subtly as to be hardly noticed at all. Still, the oak did as well as could be expected to greet each day cheerfully, shaking its many boughs with sparkle and sweetness.

The oak kept a good spirit and a love of all living things. More time passed, and the nagging emptiness still tugged at the oak at moments least expected. Through it all, through seasons bright and dark, the oak waited patiently, spreading it's boughs even further, growing roots deeper and wider from it's trunk, searching for another.

After much time had passed, the oak was old, much older than the willow was when it had elapsed, and the oak felt its spirit slip along with the breezes. So the oak tried to hold to its spirit; at least until there was a seedling nearby to share the passing with. The old lonely gnawing was working its way out from within the tree.

Finally, it got too much for the old oak to bear. He shook branches angrily, uselessly, at the wind and sun for not carrying a seedling nearby for company. The oak shook branches at the ground creatures for not being better companions and at the willow for leaving the oak. When we are most upset, sometimes we feel our pain sleet hard and cold. Leaves fell and did not grow back.

Then, one bright, warm day, two birds made their nest in the oak's boughs. At first, the oak thought of shaking the birds out, being still quite an unhappy tree. When the oak saw, however, that the birds were nesting to raise young, well, that was different and the oak thought better of it. It was good that the birds stayed, for they were songbirds, and their brood brought considerable enjoyment. The mood of the oak changed from despair to joy. The nesting birds flew with the first snow, thought not before singing the loveliest song they knew in thanks for the tree's help. Alone again, the old oak diminished.

One fierce night, as stormy a night as had ever been seen, as wild a night as had been the night the oak was seeded, thunder and lightening roared in a frightening chorus. The oak shook its branches one last time. The clouds rumbled and a sharp blue bolt of lightening struck the oak straight down the middle, splitting the trunk and sending branches crashing down in all directions. The oak passed with wildness sounding through every fiber of its being to a new self.

The next morning, all the forest was still as one by one, creatures of the ground and air bade goodbye to the oak. And birds, hundreds and hundreds of birds, took the acorns that had crowned every branch and spread them far and wide, until there were many oak seedlings growing as far as the eye could see, eager to provide companionship.   And here, in this very spot, where all around us spreads this grove of oaks, are trees that are many sons and daughters of that first oak, welcoming us with shade in the summer and kindling in the winter. For the oak did get its wish in a manner grander than had ever been hoped for, for it is the oak that is the readiest companion for us all.

Wishes Haunting Dreams

The other shadows whisper at the threshold and I hear. That around these parts, they talk about the 'Woman of the Hills', who wanders the roads keening for the lover who betrayed her. In an uncanny white gown, she roams seeking her betrothed. Those that see her turn gray overnight. Them she touches dies over a fortnight. I apologize to all them poor hearts to who she done so. I'm the one they say left her behind. Before you judge me harshly, though, listen to my tale of woe.

My people grew up soft as red clay and as loving as red wasps. So poor we thought nothing was something. We read the Bible and the JP Pearson general feed catalog from St. Louis. Wouldn'a had it, 'cepting momma made daddy take the catalog in trade for some carving work he done. It give me ideas about how wonderful St. Louis must be, I tell you now. I had two older brothers, Luke and Tom. I heard mama had a stillborn girl long 'fore I come along, but she never mentioned it. Luke took his Tennessee Music Box and looked for his fortune elsewhere. Tom left to fight wars I lost count of. Finally we got the letter and he never come back. My momma took ill after that letter and was never right again. My daddy did what he could for her, and that t'weren't much, owing as he was worn down reaping shale and limestone from what our clay would give. They both went within a few months of each other. Our place was so far back in the hills that no one even looked to buy much less put coin down.

So at fifteen I went on the road to find somethin'. I'd not find better at home, and I couldn't think I'd find worse somewhere else. I spent days walking the road out of the holler where I was bred without even seeing another human. When I slept, it was under the stars. This kept on for a mite. Lost track of how long, to be honest.

I been walking downhill for most of that morning when I heard the murmur of creek water. I went to the creek and knelt to drink. As I was having my fill I heard some branches break to the side. I stayed real still and looked to my left. A mule comes out of the brush sauntering up to the stream. He looked at me a moment, sussing me out, and then started drinking three feet past me.

There wasn't a living soul about. It wouldn't have been the first mule that had been left on his own after wandering off, or from being left behind by a family that couldn't care for him anymore. I sauntered over to him as casual as the morning fog stroking the hillside and put my hand on his neck. He moved a bit but did not bolt. All I could think was that I could ride and save my legs a mite when a voice spoke out from beyond the trees.

"You in the habit of stealin' mules?"

It was the voice of a girl and the eyes of a woman. She stepped out into view. Hair braided by sunrise, eyes as blue as deep water. I forgot to breathe, forgot to make my heart beat. If I hadn't been holding onto the mule, it would have been the creek for me.

"You in the habit on sneakin' up on folks minding their own doings?" I heard my voice squack.

She stepped out further into the clearing, wearing a hand patched dress of red and black. She made my head swim and my body ache like a tooth gone bad, like the sweetest cake you'd ever eat. She looked at me curious, like she'd never laid eyes on a man before. I stepped back to the creek and got me a gulp. I pulled myself up and tried to stare her down. I wiped my mouth and hoped I looked braver than I was. She stood still looking at me like I was cow with a duck's bill, not saying anything else. She part twirled to her right and left, never taking her eyes away.

"I guess maybe you were mindin' your own concerns." She said. She didn't sound like she really thought that true.

"I'm Bo Ledbetter." I held out my hand.

For a flash it was like she got smaller. It was like she pulled herself deeper into her.

"I'm Rose Clannard." She didn't offer any part of her arm. "What are you doing out here?"

"I'm moving' through. Headed for St. Louis."

"That's too far away."

She shot me a look like she was aiming a varmint rifle.

"I bet you don't get there."

It wasn't like she was teasing – more like hoping.

"This your mule?" I asked.

"My granna's."

"You think she'd barter for him?"

Rose laughed.

"What you got to trade beside your looks?"

"I can work – do whatever you need doing. Work from sun to sun as you see fit."

She thought for a while, still staring, still weaving to her own inside tune.

"You'd better come on with me then."

Rose sashayed into the brush, which seemed to move aside for her a bit so her dress wouldn't get caught on the brambles or branches. It was deep woods we were in – the sun grew dimmer though it weren't even mid day. She knew the woods. She moved through them seeing things as clear as if she was in a meadow. As we walked the sky clouded up and I could feel rain skim my face. I could also feel my stomach and hoped we'd see a fruit tree or some such thing to eat.

We kept moving, following a path I could only see once or twice. It mighta been a tick trail, big as it was. She looked back once or twice to make sure I was still with her. We were in deep woods now, trees so big around two grown men reaching around the trunks couldn't touch fingers. Moss was everywhere. Even the air had a dark green look to it. The further in we got, the quieter it got. Even though it was a bright day, under the branches it was dusk. The mule followed us, but I had a feeling that it was not his first choice.

We come out into a clearing. The air was sweet, like honeysuckle. There was a cool breeze that took the sweat off my head and made me feel happier than I could remember. On the top of a hill was a house that we made towards.

"This is my home. I expect mamma and granna can find you something to stop that growling I've been listening to for the last hour."

Around the house was a ring of mushrooms, close enough that the mushroom lids almost touched. I remembered my daddy saying that if I saw something like that, I should skedaddle. My stomach wasn't in any mood to hold to that notion. I stepped on the porch and heard chiming, like a church that was over in the next hill. I looked for it and saw some pieces of glass tied to a string, playing in the wind. It was the prettiest sound I'd ever heard. It was a song I knew and for the life of me couldn't recollect. There were footsteps behind me.

"Rose, did you bring home another stray?"

The voice behind me was like the glass song, pretty as a bluebird and sweet as a spring rain. I turned and saw a woman who could have been Rose's sister, except for the laugh lines around her eyes and mouth. She had hair red as dawn that come near to her hips. She was wiping her hands on an apron. There was dirt on her dress and I knew she'd been in a garden.

"Momma, this here is Bo Ledbetter, on his way to St. Louis, or so he tells. I thought we could feed him before we send him on his way." Rose looked sweet at me and it took my breath. With the same kind of reckoning eye Rose used, her ma looked me over.

"Can you do chores?"

"Yes'm. Whatever you got to do."

She pointed with her thumb over her should to a shed where an axe sat next to a pile of medium sized logs.

"I don't feed idlers. Get us wood for the stove and we'll see what we can rustle up for you. That suit you?"

"Yes'm."

It took me about an hour to get the wood down. As I brung the last of the wood over it struck me that I'd seen a pool a bit behind the shed. I went down to wash the sweat and dirt off. I felt much better coming out, until I couldn't find my clothes. Instead, where I'd left them, was a bundle. Somehow, I knew I weren't there by my lonesome. Just as the thought come to me, there was a little rustle in a privet bush a skip or two away. Rose was watchin', my bones told me.

I walked over naked as the truth and opened them up. Inside was a man's flannel shirt, a little big for me, but it wore good. There was also a pair of trousers that fit me better. I pulled on my shoes, which to my woe had not been taken, and walked back to the house. I heard Rose whisper and then she was walkin' next to me.

"You watch me get dressed?"

Rose watched me for a second, her eyes looking in me, as familiar with me as I was. And I felt I knew her right back. She smiled at me like honeysuckle blooming and took my hand as we headed for her house.

The aroma of biscuits and taters wrapped around me and walked me in the house like a mother leading a child by the hand. Rose and her momma looked at me and smiled. In the corner an older woman worked a loom, not paying me a bit of mind. In the window ledge behind her was a bunch of herbs growing. Presently she looked my way.

"This the lumberjack what tried to walk off with Sadie?" Her voice was flint, but her eyes were playful.

"Yes, granna."

"Best have him sit down and eat, then."

Let me tell you that were one of the best meals I ever had. Biscuits with apple butter, fried onions and taters, washed down with goat milk. I had two full plates and argued with my stomach over having a third. The ladies had already finished and were over in the corner, Rose and her mamma sitting on the floor around her granna, who was sitting in her rocker and occasionally looking at me. Rose got up and walked over.

"Did you enjoy your meal?"

"Better than stringy rabbit on a spit. Can't recollect last time I ate so good."

"We been talking. We need someone to help out for the season. We can't pay but a few coins a month. You interested?"

It didn't take me longer than a scratch on my chin to say yes. My life became real steady for a while. So steady that as one season turned to the next I kept on finding work to do and reasons to stay.

During the days I'd build sheds or fix the house or plant or reap. I'd see Rose come by me doing her chores, and I'd hew a little harder, dig a little deeper. We'd work together, smelling each other, and both get a bit more flushed. We'd take our meals, and our hands would find a reason to touch under the table. All the while we got closer; I kept thinking it would wither someway. I knew that come from my own ways comin' up. What really got me sweating was the ways Rose had me feeling. She was as nice to me as a cool breeze on a dog day. The way I was feeling for her was butterfly light one clock tick, then the next I'd be scared knowing someone had my heart that easy. Some nights, trying to sort myself out, I couldn't sleep easy. I felt like I had a gravel comforter under me.

Most evenings I'd listen to Rose sing whilst her momma played a zither and her granna played a psaltery. Prettier music I never heard in any church and the songs they sung were full of heat and life. Songs about the woods, about men and women with all sorts of unusual ways about 'em. Songs about lovers proving themselves with questions and quests. I felt them as real as if they were in front of me. Her grandma knew more tales than trees have leaves.

Rose's mamma knew more about plants than anyone I'd ever met. Rose and I would follow her into the woods as she looked for ginseng or truffles or other roots. She taught me which plants would heal and which would harm. She taught me how to watch animals and birds to know what the weather would do the next day. Rose's granna taught me a lot too. She could take a set of playing cards and tell me more about myself than I thought anyone knew. She knew more about my ma and pa and brothers than I ever told anyone. She sewed me up some right nice shirts and pants, using bits and pieces of whatever fabric turned up.

One day we was sitting on the porch watching a real pretty sunset. I said "I wish I could put that sunset in my pocket and keep it to look at whenever I got cold and lonely." She looked at me real deep for a moment and said: "There are the things we wish for, and then there are things we have no idea we were wishing for that find us. Until they come to us, it's those things that come and haunt us in our dreams." I didn't know then what she meant. It was a few months later that I learned to see her meaning.

Those times I wasn't working or spending time with Rose's mamma and granna I spent with Rose. We walked and talked. Mainly it was me talking about what a good mamma and granna she had. My feelings for Rose grew too during all this time. Every night we slept pallet next to pallet. I'd listen to her breathe or turn over and my heart told me this was where I was supposed to be. My head, though, my head still wanted to get to St. Louis. And another part of my head was just plain scared about Rose and the hold she had on me. I spun like an elm seed fallin' to ground. I figured I'd talk to Rose, 'bout St Louis, anyway. I just didn't know how to talk about the ways I felt for her.

We made our way to the edge of the pond, where she'd left that change of clothes for me once. I started talkin' 'bout the JP Pearson catalog and the kind of place I figured St. Louis must be. With all I'd learned here, I told her, I knew I'd make me good money, more than just a few coins a months. I even heard myself, to my terror and delight, say she might think about comin' along. Rose listened to me, to what I was thinking. When I finished, she drew her knees up under her chin and watched the water for a long while.

"I druther you stay than I go. There's nothing in St. Louis that I want – nothing that would mean more to me than what I have here."

"You'd have my word I'd try to make it back to you. Isn't that worth something?"

"Worth?"

The word stung me like a hornet and hung round my head like cold dew.

"If I ain't worthy of you in this here and now, then when will I be? Don't you leave me, Bo Ledbetter. I won't ever give up lookin' for you. And grief be upon them what might stand in my way."

She stood up suddenly and disappeared into the woods.

I walked back to the house thinking about Rose, about staying or going, about what I wanted.

That night dinner didn't have the sort of talk I was used to. After dinner I went onto the porch to catch the last rays of sunset and Rose's mamma joined me.

"Rose wants you to stay. She feels real deep for you." She paused. "There ain't nothing for you anywhere but here."

"I feel deep for her too.' I waited for the words to clear my throat. "But St. Louis's got me reeled like a catfish."

"You could find a place here. You made yourself real useful. Stay a while until the weather warms up. Stay until you get your head clear."

"If I don't reach St. Louis now, somethin' tells me I never will. I can always come back. I'm set on this."

Rose's mamma looked at me like a bad fork on a hard road.

"You might not be able to find us again. We're – far back."

"If I can get to St. Louis, I can get back to here."

She looked back toward the cabin, then stared at me.

"When are you thinking of going?"

"Maybe I oughta get at first light. It won't get any easier for Rose or me the longer I put it off."

That morning, before light touched the hills, I put together what little I had and lit out. Rose's mamma and her grandma met me at the edge of the clearing.

"We have a way for you to go." Rose's grandma said. "It'll save you a long walk."

They led me a different way than Rose and I came, further up into the hills. In the darkness I could see a cabin or some such. It looked like just the ivy around it held it up.

"This is a special place,' Rose's mamma said, 'we want to show it to you before you go."

We came onto the porch. Rose's mamma and grandma started to speak together, real soft. It was like a prayer, but it made me feel chilled and the hairs on my neck stood up.

As we came into the single room, Rose's grandma lit a candle. The room was empty. All the same, the light the candle cast on the walls seemed to reach out to me, to the women with me. Moaning like a hard wind circled round my feet and rose toward my head.

"We think you should stay here for a spell until you clear your head." Rose's mamma said this with a love I'd gotten to know and with a sadness I wasn't used to and lit another candle.

The two women spread their hands and said something in a tongue I'd never heard. With a flash the two candle flickers became one bright vine that run around me like a creeper round cedar.

I felt something, bit by bit. I felt myself being pulled into the wall, into the shadows on the wall. Rose's mamma and grandma seemed to fade and become hazy. I struggled to get out, but I couldn't pull away from the cedar. I couldn't come away from the wall.

"You'll be safe here." Rose's granna said. She looked at me with a light in her eyes I'd never seen in anyone afore. That gaze of hers started to core my soul like I was an apple. I turned away to find Rose's ma looking the exact same way into me. It was like they were cutting the seams keeping my spirit to my body.

"There, there," they both said softly, though I never saw their mouths move. "If we didn't think so much of you we wouldn't have brought you here. Here you won't get cold, or hungry, or lonely. When we think it's right, we'll let her know where you are, and she can come and sit with you. Won't that be nice? Meanwhile, you can get to know the suitors we liked best that courted us and tried to leave. Once you're settled, we'll come and visit"

I tried to say something but my voice came out as a flicker of shadow. The women left, left me alone with the other shadows on the wall.

So that's where I am now; I don't know why they haven't yet told Rose where I was. Every time one of the other came, they just looked older and older and never brought Rose. It seems forever since either of them came, and I dare not wonder why.

I don't know why Rose could never find me. In the time I been here, she's never found me. The other shadows tell me that Rose died before she was old enough to know about me, but I don't feel it. Shadows don't feel

Maybe some time, if you find yourself back in hills you never thought you'd find your way to, you might find this cabin.

Just don't light the candle.

Still Life

The child thought that she could feel angels holding her. She felt a soft pink glow all around her, like the softest cotton she'd ever known. She tried to remember all her grannah had told her about angels. She remembered the sounds of fresh baked bread and the warm aroma of wind chimes. She evoked the sight of herself curled up in her grandmother's lap, swaying in the rocker. Her grandmother was softly singing one of her pretty songs with made up words. She asked her grannah about the song with her inquisitive eyes.

"The song's about blessed spirits, Lila. They come to help us. People all around the world see them."

"But where do they come from grannah? Why won't they let us see them?"

Her grandmother gently moved the strawberry blonde bangs from Lila's lake blue eyes. Lila loved it when her grandmother cleared the hair from her eyes.

"Maybe it's not so much we can't see them. Maybe we don't want to see. Maybe there are all sorts of things people don't want to see."

"Why not?"

"Some people, when they see things they don't think are supposed to be real, decide not to see them at all."

"What sort of things?" Lila wasn't sure she wouldn't be a little frightened hearing this; at six that part of life's road map is marked with darkness and the mean sounds in its night. She knew her grannah would make sure she was safe, so she relaxed a bit.

"Things that aren't supposed to be there. Ways people aren't supposed to act. Feelings they're not supposed to have. Thoughts they're not supposed to think."

Lila laughed.

"How can you be scared of that?"

Now Lila wondered if she had stopped feeling things she was supposed to. She wasn't scared, not anymore. She had stopped crying a while ago. She wasn't mad that everything had happened, although it terrified her at first. Even the hurt was gone. She was sleepy. Every time she closed her eyes, the bright came a little nearer, got a little bigger. Lila felt the pink glow cover her like a warm bath.

Then she was gone.

Floyd gnawed on what was left of his pinky fingernail and felt the harsh gaze from the other side of the bars.

The general hung high on the wall, looking into the cell, judgmental and stern. James Madison Cook's name was engraved on the shiny plate attached to the frame. Floyd was sure the nameplate was brass. Nothing gold around these parts lasted long. Floyd supposed that he was a great-great grand daddy of one of the sheriffs who had stomped these grounds long years past. Someone must have dug the painting out from storage and hung it since the last time Floyd was in the hoosegow.

Floyd stroked his chin as he looked at the painting as if he was staring into a mirror.

"We do take after each other a bit." Floyd realized with a start. The same hawk noses and black Irish eyes sat on both men. Even though he could see only tuffs or rust red hair under the General's hat, Floyd fancied that Cook had the same cowlick he had, seeing as how their other features matched up.

An eternally inert hound dog sat beside the great man, who held his hand over the dog, ready to strike the cur if he dared opened his mouth to bark. The dog gazed at him in devoted fear. The general no doubt had scared everyone who knew him while he lived and probably scared most folks who considered him from behind the bars.

Floyd didn't think of himself as most folks.

"Whaddya looking so glum for?" Floyd said out loud. "You ain't behind these bars."

He wanted a smoke. He wanted a swig. He wanted out. He wanted something to happen, something different than the void he was used to feeling.

If he hadn't run across that checkpoint, if he had remembered that his license had been suspended, if he hadn't let the deputy check his car, those panties would never have been found and they wouldn't have started asking questions.

Floyd had no answers that satisfied the unusually grim deputy, and he had been arrested there. Floyd didn't know about the girl then, but, brother, after near a straight day of being questioned by Sheriff Dawkins, and threatened by Pullman, he sure knew about her now. He damn near knew more than the police about the case.

Floyd knew things would go easier for him if he had been able to tell the sheriff where the girl was. If he told what he really knew, they'd know Floyd was just in jail for the three squares and bed.

Weren't any way he could show them where that girl was at. He had a feeling it wouldn't do her no good no mind anyhow. He figured to be better off letting them think the worst. Once it went before a judge he'd be out and then he could figure out where he'd stay next. For once Floyd's reputation was working in his behalf.

He had hoped Jeff was still working at the jail. He had counted on it because Jeff could be counted on to carry in a jug now and again and to let Floyd get fresh air once a day or so. Jeff had taken sick and Harold had been put there.

Harold was a hard as an Osage orange tree that wouldn't let a tick get away with a crawl. Floyd knew him when he was still known as 'Rhino', when his bulk and his sharpness brought in many a moonshiner and poacher.

Harold, and before that his people, had hauled in Floyd, his brothers and his daddy, plus his daddy's kin, to jail on many an occasion.

Now Harold was physically threadbare, a once spectacular tree worn winter withered. He heard the half shuffle and kick step of Harold approaching his cell as his smoke ravaged voice brought Floyd back to his present.

"Someone to see you, Craiven."

A woman, a good-looking woman with dark hair and a busty figure, stopped in front of his cell. Floyd hadn't seen a woman this good for a long while. She was dressed in denim shorts and a tee shirt advertising a bluegrass festival from a few years back. She looked like she had just thrown on the first things she found. She looked distracted.

"Please – what's happened to - to Lila?"

He looked at her curiously.

"My daughter."

That was when Floyd saw her eyes. Reddened, dark half circles. She'd not had much sleep because she'd been crying. The girl's mother, he guessed. He decided to try the truth for a change.

"Ma'am, they got the wrong man in here. I wouldn't hurt a fly."

"Sheriff Dawkins says they've got evidence that shows Lila was in your car."

"If they do, ma'am, someone else put it there. I got no idea what happened to your daughter."

She looked at him deep, they way someone might look into a crystal mirror to gain answers to hidden questions. He could tell she didn't think much of the answers she saw.

"You might think you can slip away, mister. You might think the law will be on your side, or that you can cover your tracks enough to keep out of the penitentiary or from the needle. Let you tell something, mister. You didn't just take a little girl. You have bothered people you oughta not messed with."

Floyd, smarting from her tone, turned and spit in the cell. The words were out of his mouth before he considered them. Floyd had always been quick off the handle when he was pushed a little.

"Let me tell you something, missy. I don't know what happened to your little bitch. I don't care what happened to her. If something happened to her maybe she deserved it. Maybe the wrong person came by and she bit them in the ass. Whatever happened to her is your concern, not mine. And if you come back to see me again, you should wear something that shows me a little more of your tits, if you wanna do me any favors."

Her face paled and her mouth dropped, gaping like a raven. She turned and walked off. Floyd amused himself thinking that his words stung her like hers stung him.

He felt Harold's glare burn his neck and looked at him insolently.

"You might not have wanted to talk to her like that." Harold grated.

"And why is that?"

"Her people – Her name's Cunningham' – Harold waited so Floyd could indicate whether or not he knew the Cunninghams. Harold shrugged indifferently. Harold glowered and continued.

"Her mother's people - the Sonorias. They mess with the old ways from what I hear."

Floyd shook his head. He knew that Harold believed in that ol' back in the hollow mumble jumble. He could do without it himself. He chortled at Harold's naivety.

"Rhino, you been sippin' your apple jack behind the cell block again?"

Floyd guffawed with such enjoyment that Harold rapped the bars with his nightstick and continued.

"Remember old Miser Evans, the one who owned the store on the Fellbright hollow road?"

Floyd replied with an apathetic shrug.

"I maybe mighta snuck in once or twice after closing. Years ago, when I was fulla snot and attitude"

Harold glared, then went on.

"Old woman Sonoria had her house up that little access road by his store, had this big old oak tree on it. Evans cut it down without her permission so folks could see his store from the state road. She was real hot about it – called the sheriff to get Evans put in jail. 'Course, that was when McInereny was sheriff and he never did check into it."

Floyd spun his fingers in an exasperated circle. Harold narrowed his eyes.

"Well, then, not too long later, Evans got hisself killed in a robbery, and you know he'd never been held up in fifty years of ownin' that store. Talk was she'd put the whammy on him."

"I don't recollect any of this. Where was I?"

"This all come about when you were in that work camp upstate. After Evans died, she gave the place to her daughter and lit out to the woods. Ain't no one hardly seen her since then."

Harold stopped to search his memory. A brief nod told Floyd that Harold had finished his chronicle, as he looked off into the distance of the past, blind to the present.

"Let Harold go on a bit and he'll tell you about the hell hound with blazing black eyes down in Poorhouse Hollow."

The voice was as granite as its owner

Floyd stepped;'''''',m to one side and saw Dawkins behind Rhino. His mother had named him 'Chris'. His father had named him 'Harley' and that was that. Most folks just called him Dawkins, unless they were on the wrong end of his wrath. Then it was 'Sheriff'. Dawkins was a few years younger than Floyd. For years he had farmed tobacco. When the crops went bust after the government buy-out, he made money farming organic tobacco. When the money didn't balance the back breaking work, Dawkins, being a smart man, looked around. He saw how poorly folks thought of Jimmy

McInnery, who had been sheriff since Dawkins was a boy. McInnery had his fingers in nearly every pie and many other folks hands in his pockets. Dawkins was well known and better trusted and so traded in his topper for a badge. With his bald head and strong man build, he looked more like Mr. Clean than Mr. Law.

Dawdling like a turtle on an abandoned back road, Harold reached inside his vest and pulled out a silver pocket watch, engraved with a railroad train. The lid creaked as he opened it to check the time. Floyd knew Harold's father, who had gotten it from his daddy, had given Harold the watch. Floyd wanted to take the watch and smash it beneath his shoe. Harold glanced up from his watch and grinned at Floyd, his head cocked to the side as if hearing him in his mind. He slipped the watch back into his pocket, still giving Floyd a smile that made Floyd uncomfortable.

"Guess Judge Hollis be startin' his court anytime. Ready to go?"

Harold opened the cell door. Floyd saw Harold's hand firmly on the handle of his pistol. Harold may have lost a step in strength and speed, but neither skill was needed to shoot Floyd dead and Harold could still do that.

As he started down the hallway, Floyd squinted at the bright sky he could see through the window at the end of the hall.

"I need my shades."

"Don't rightly know where they at right now. Guess you'll just have to squint."

Floyd felt his heart palpitate and swallowed to calm himself down as the left the jail house. He walked with Harold the short distance across the square to the courthouse. The sun hurt Floyd's eyes. The sun had always hurt his eyes. When he was young, he was frequently left to watch the stills. He would ask for something to shade his eyes. A hat or some dark spectacles. His daddy would let out a laugh that brought more pain than comfort.

"You ain't man enough to wear no hat, boy. The sheriff come round here, he'll see that hat and shoot you for fishin' bait. Naw, you just use your hand. Sides, better for you to get used to looking afar with your own peepers."

So he had watched, alone, for intruders. Floyd spent as much of his childhood watching as much as he could, then he decided he had to make up for that lost living. Living while folks who considered themselves 'respectable' got mad at him doing the things they could only wish they could do. He knew them. They were the people who stared at him from inside the shops. Who watched from the café along the square. Or the ones standing around the courthouse entrance waiting for him. Floyd did not as much see as sense the looks from them. He had, for as far as his memory spanned, felt their belittling looks, their tsk-tsking pitying, and their feeling of superiority. He was proud and held his head even with the rest of them. Yet they could claim one facet of living that he could not. They belonged somewhere, to someone.

Floyd had been on his own by the time he was twelve. His mom had been taken with tick fever and died when he was barely out of diapers. His dad and granddad, left to their choices, preferred to run shine and live wild. If Floyd wanted to stay in the family, he had to keep up; they didn't slow down for anyone – not kin, not friend. When the cancer ate away his granddad when he was ten, he didn't shed a tear. Neither did his father. When his dad lost a drunken dare to beat a slow freight on a slick night three years later he turned to the only life he knew.

He made no excuses and offered no apologies. If he got caught fair and square he took it as cool as stream stone in the shade. He never took from anyone didn't have

"So ends all who would follow Satan's ways!"

Floyd didn't recognize the voice; when he turned to face the accuser, he found himself looking into the reddened face of a heavy-set middle aged woman wearing a pink pulled wool suit. He smiled what he thought was a neighborly enough smile. She responded by spitting in his face.

"Sister, we mustn't turn our back on the fallen and forgotten. Jesus has a place for them in his plan."

Floyd knew the voice of Brother Jeremiah Falls, a relative newcomer to town, having only been there for a decade. He had come into town, knowing no one, and bought an abandoned church. Falls had an iron core inside his downy coat. All by himself, he had rebuilt and rejuvenated the church, bringing back its sense of welcome and then wonders, as the pews started to fill with the faithful. Most of the townsfolk had taken to calling him 'Brother', owing to the fact he was not ordained. He had developed a strong congregation, based on his energy and unwavering belief that only the chosen few would survive any vague, upcoming apocalypse. Because God kept an open line to them, and he and his worshippers would do the main choosing, these lambs were only meek in name; their wrath and spite could cook a chicken at forty paces. They made

Floyd laugh. They made Floyd crazy. He wished that he could smash them all, leaving the Brother for last. He wanted the Brother to see what kind of nightmares Floyd had grown up with – to experience them first hand.

Without realizing, Floyd's wrists strained against the cuffs. Harold, his eyes narrowing, saw what was happening and moved his hand back to his pistol.

They entered the dank shade of the courthouse and went upstairs. The walls were a dead yellow. The stairs were so narrow; Floyd led Harold into the courtroom and to the prisoner's area. Floyd held his hands up so that Harold could unlock then reattach the handcuffs to the steel post that braced the wooden beam that bordered the seating area.

Floyd watched the rest of the people on the docket enter and find seats. Folks dressed better than they would for church, or to apply for a job. Some folks were still sticky mouthed bleary from a night spent drinking. Floyd leaned back in the bench and closed his eyes. No one was going to make him lose his control.

Johnny McGavock, his public defender, entered, saw him, and approached him. McGavock's legs always seemed to lead his torso, as if his upper half was reluctant to move. McGavock ran his hand through his shock of brown hair. Floyd thought he looked like a matchstick with hair. Still, Floyd reasoned, he was free.

"We caught a huge break." McGavock said conspiratorially.

"We?" Floyd spat back. "You ain't doing any time if I get sent up."

'Look – just don't say anything and with any luck, you'll be sleeping in your own bed tonight-." McGavock paused. "Look – I tried to get your landlord to let you back in. I promise, though – we'll find you something."

McGavock looked behind him as the bailiff called the court to order. He went and sat in the attorney's area as Judge William Hollis entered. The judge was relatively young for such an important post. Floyd thought that judges should be old, stern, and senile. Hollis was virile, solicitous and cunning. Floyd sat through the docket, mentally assessing their hick factor as each defendant was called before the bench. When they came to his case, McGavock moved for dismissal.

"According to the state's own forensics, the garments found in Mr. Craiven's car did not contain any DNA. For all the state knows, the defendant bought the garment for-

"

McGavock paused and looked to Floyd. Judge Hollis observed this and addressed Floyd.

"Mr. Craiven, why did you have girl's underwear –"

"Objection, your Honor. Inflammatory."

"Counselor, I'm just calling a duck a duck here. You simmer down. Objection overruled. Mr. Craiven?"

Floyd knew his answer.

"Your honor, I had 'em to check my oil."

"Your oil, Mr. Craiven?"

"Yessir. You know how hard it is to find wipes at the gas station anymore. I was in a hurry and went into the Dollar Store and they were the first thing I found, so I bought 'em. Did it just before I got pulled over."

Hollis, looking with irritation at the prosecutor, scratched his head.

"What else do you have to hold Mr. Craiven, Mr. Pullman?

The heavyset prosecutor pulled at his ill fitting vest, and then wiped his high forehead.

"Your honor', Pullman began in his squeaky voice. 'We firmly believe that the defendant is guilty of this horrendous crime against the community –"

"What evidence does the state have of his guilt in this crime?" McGavock chimed in.

"Well, Mr. Pullman?" Hollis added in a voice that suggested his day was becoming longer than he had hoped.

Pullman pulled at his collar and looked over to Sheriff Dawkins. At the moment, he looked like someone who had just been caught committing an act of animal husbandry with the wrong animal.

"Sheriff Dawkins?" Hollis inquired politely, though his voice was beginning to show strain.

"Yer honor, y'see, we known Craiven a long time, known his family."

Pullman interrupted Dawkins.

"He's sure as shi- shooting got sumpthin' to do with that poor little girl going missing. Everyone knows it."

"The law doesn't know it, sir. Not unless you have evidence to prove it."

Pullman tugged at his collar, which was quickly becoming wetter by the second. Hollis sat imperiously watching everyone involved, tapping his fingers on the dais. Pullman looked at Dawkins for help. Dawkins, having been shut up once by the prosecutor, ignored him and sat silent, watching Judge Hollis preside over this quickly dissipating preliminary trial.

"Mr. Pullman, is there any other evidence the state wishes to present at this time?"

"Your honor, if the court would indulge me for a second –"

"It's a yes or no question, Mr. Pullman."

Pullman breathed so deeply Floyd thought he'd suck the air right out of the courthouse.

"No, your honor."

"Then I'm dismissing this case without prejudice. When you have your facts straight you may bring Mr. Craiven back before me. Mr. Craiven, you're free to go – I would not leave this jurisdiction if I were you, sir."

The sound of Hollis's gavel rung like a church bell in Floyd's ears. He fairly leapt from the bench seat, leaning over to shake McGavock's hand. As Harold unlocked the handcuffs, Floyd looked through some of the faces in the courtroom, his eyes dismissing onlookers with the high and mighty glare of the vindicated. He turned to leave the courtroom, purposefully avoiding the shocked steel gaze of the girl's mother. He could see her from the corner of his eye, as she approached Dawkins and Pullman.

Diane Cunningham wrenched taut from the inside out so she could deal with this new assault. The deadened voice she heard address Pullman was a logjam in the rage she wanted to feel. The torrents she wanted to bottle.

"You told me that you were certain that man killed my child. And you can't even prove it at a trial." Diane, feeling the heat of her face rise, wasn't sure if she wanted to cry or who she wanted to kill.

Dawkins, moving his eyes away from Diane's direct line of sight, felt the familiar acid churning in him of the thing not set right. He felt for the woman. Virtually every moment of his time not spent on sleeping or bathing was focused on finding the child and her assailant. He had run out of places to look and people to ask.

No one had seen the child as she walked along the road the quarter mile to her house from a friend's house. Dawkins had tracked her movements the entire day from when she woke up to the time around noon when her mother had given her permission to wait for her friend Casey in the front yard of their home. Apparently Casey had run late and Lila had decided to walk there by herself, which she had done many times before with her mother. Ross Tucker, who lived a few doors from the Cunninghams, saw Lila stand in front of the fence and look down toward Casey's house. That was the last anyone had seen of her. Dawkins had spent days talking to the people living all up and down the road, going back and forth more than five miles in both directions, searching for signs of the girl or of foul play.

While he did that, Pullman focused his efforts on dealing with the press. He soon started referring to the investigation when it when well as "My investigation." When it went poorly, it was "Dawkins' investigation." Dawkins didn't care one or the other. He cared that that girl and her family had no peace of mind.

Pullman pulled himself into a press friendly 'comfort the family' pose and addressed Diane with all the sensitivity he could simulate.

"Ms. Cunningham, I wouldn't worry about this. We've still got some shells in the revolver of justice."

"How dare you." Her voice hit hard as forged steel.

"Ms. Cunningham –'

"No – you listen to me. Don't you dare throw pathetic sound bites at me. If this man did it, prove it. If he didn't – get who did."

The comment she hurled at Pullman stung Dawkins like a slap to the face.

Diane was unlocking her car when she felt a hand on her shoulder. Already angry, she turned to give the person an oral shellacking, and held her invective when she saw it was Brother Falls. She cleared her throat to sweep the desolation from her mouth.

"I want to thank you for the way your congregation has offered its help. You've been . . . very kind."

"I wanted to make sure you were taken care of. None of us could know what you've gone through losing your girl like you did. Though there's also – well . ."

Diane sensed Falls measuring the moment.

"I know how hard it must have been for you to grow up, your mother being like she is."

"My mother? Like she is-? What do you mean?"

She looked confused; then she frowned as she understood what Falls meant.

"My mother not attending church services. That's what you're talking about."

"We just want what's best for her. She needs to get on God's good path."

"My mother is generous and kind to everyone she meets. Isn't there some book that says something like 'what you do for the least of us you do for me.' Isn't that on God's good path?"

Falls shook his head emphatically.

"There's more to being righteous than how you treat others. It's following God's word – behaving as he proscribes. Those things are far more important."

"Important to who? Follow God's word according to who - you? Follow God's word by way of the gossipy clucks that come to church two days a week to make themselves feel better about being hypocrites the rest of the week?"

Falls paused for a moment, reaching for the truth that would persuade Diane.

"We accept those sincere in their search for righteousness, even if they stumble along the path. We would welcome you – or your mother – if you want to find redemption."

"I won't speak for my mother. For me – well, as I said; I truly thank everyone at your church for your thoughts and care. If you want me to come to services, I'll come to thank the congregation. But I won't be emotionally coerced by you out of some imaginary debt of guilt."

"We'll continue to pray for you, sister."

"Look – let's agree – I'll concern myself with my salvation if you concern yourself with yours."

Brother Falls stared at her with a look midway between sympathy and scorn. Diane got in and started the engine. She didn't want to break down. Not there. Not with the brother watching oh so solicitously. She turned on the CD player and rode out of town. It was a mix disk, something she used to love to do, putting songs together for friends. As she sped down the road Eva Cassidy's version of "Time after Time" came on.

"If you're lost you can look
And you will find me . . .
If you fall I will catch you,

I'll be waiting"

That was all she could take. She pulled onto the side of the road, killed the engine, while leaving the battery running so she could listen as she put her head on the steering wheel and sobbed desperately. She hated everyone and everything with a fury she barely recognized as hers. She never should have let Lila wait in the yard alone for Casey's mom to pick her up.

All the way back to the jail Floyd didn't think of the sun, hardly minded it at all. All he thought about was getting that drink. He knew vaguely that he had to find a place to stay the night, though he wasn't thinking that far ahead. If it meant not having to spend any more time with Harold, he'd sleep in the woods.

Once back at the jail, he said his fare-thee-well to his cell and to the General and went to the booking desk. He looked inside the property envelope containing the items he had on him when arrested. He was headed toward the door when Harold called from behind him.

"Got a lot of angry folks waitin' down by the front door. Brother Falls can't right keep them folks calm. They all in a right strong whirl. Sheriff says we should take you out in a car till you get past the crowd."

Floyd, not entirely comfortable with the idea of being chauffeured by the sheriff's boys, saw none too many options for anything else. He prepared himself for the worst.

When he saw who would be taking him to wherever he wanted to go, he felt better. Tommy and Billy Boarson were two good ol' boys who he used to ride with when they were all teenagers. Back then there wasn't much they weren't up for. He wasn't sure who had done more to find trouble, him or Billy and Tommy. The Boarsons were almost like brothers and he was glad to see them.

They stood outside by one of the sheriff's cars. They stood alert, wild black hair and black eyes atop lean farmer's bodies.

He went down the back stairs, where the offices were and passed Judy, the receptionist, who gave him a knowing smile.

'Girl', he thought, 'I'll be coming back to look you up.'

The car was running and Tommy and Billy were standing at either end, keeping an eye out for anyone watching them. Floyd dove into the back seat.

"C'mon – let's get out of here." Floyd said impatiently. Tommy got in the driver's side while Billy took the shotgun seat. With a nod Tommy started up the car and they pulled away from the parking lot.

Once they had left the town limits, Floyd sat up and stretched his arms. He saw Billy bend over and get something from under the passenger seat. He turned back toward Floyd with a wide grin and a bottle of Jack Daniel Red.

"Thought you deserved something special." Billy tossed the bottle over the seat. Floyd caught it one handed, cracked open the top and took a long swig in one smooth motion.

Tommy, watching in the rear view mirror, chortled.

"Yew ain't lost a step, you summbitch!"

Floyd brought down the bottle for a satisfied sigh and a loud belch.

"Better believe it, turdhead! This bottle is fine for me, but what are you all gonna drink?"

They all laughed at that. Billy pulled out another bottle, this one Jack Black, and he and Tommy passed that between them. Floyd sat back and relaxed, nursing his bottle as he thought about where he was gonna sleep that night. There were some houses that had no one in them – where families had moved or had left the house in order to build a new home or put up a double wide. He paid no attention to the brothers in the front seat, who were arguing about something.

"It's not this road, asswipe – we gotta go past the old Kitchner place, like I told yew half hour ago!"

"n' I'm telling yew the road's been worked on since then. Ya can't get nowhere by goin' that way."

Billy turned to speak to Floyd.

"We're on our way to get some dew – get us real shit faced - and find you a place to get some shuteye. Just lay back and we'll wake you when we get there."

"I'm in you boys good hands. As long it's dry and warm and has some willin' gal, I'm happy."

Floyd took a long swig to finish the bottle, closed his eyes and let the rhythm of the car lull him to a dozy sleep.

He didn't know what time or where he was when the car came to a stop. All he knew was that it was so dark he wasn't sure if his eyes were open or not until the flashlight nearly blinded him.

"Damn, boys', he yelled, trying to blink the after light image away from inside his eyelids, 'a simple tug on m'leg would've woke me up just fine!"

"Time to get out, Floyd, we're here." There was something in Billy's voice that made Floyd nervous. Floyd told himself it was the oncoming sounds of the thunderstorm he heard in the distance that made him feel so. Floyd hated storms. Floyd did as he was told and slid out of the car, dropping the empty bottle onto the ground as he tried to stand steady. He found that near impossible and staggered a couple of yards away, using the light of the flashlight to guide him and picked up a tree limb to help steady him.

The road was hard to see in the dark, though the flashlights made it easy to find his way. Floyd couldn't see the lights of any house nearby. The road was so narrow it barely spanned the car. A bit up the road, Floyd could barely make out the silhouette of an old logging road forking off into the trees to the right. He felt Tommy's hand on his shoulder as Tommy spoke with something like reluctance in his voice.

"Floyd, a lot happened to all of us through the years. We've grown up, got families, found good jobs, found something to hang our hats on, if you know what I mean."

"Tommy, you lettin' your liquor get your tongue again?"

"Tommy's trying to give you one last chance to see the error of your ways, Floyd." Billy still had that hard edge to his voice. The thunder neared. Floyd could see lightning flare the sky and could see by its flash that Billy and Tommy had something in mind. Floyd started to feel less threatened by the storm and more by the brothers.

"How's bout we find that place we were headed to and keep dry?" Floyd tried to keep his voice level, confident he could talk his way out of whatever the brothers had in mind. He walked between them toward the car. Probably had a mind to leave him out here to walk back in the rain. They probably meant to –

The first blow caught him in the small of the back, driving him to his knees. The limb flew from his hands, too far for him to use as a weapon. Billy kicked in the stomach, making him throw up the whiskey he had drunk as he rolled over and lay flat on his back. Floyd tried to catch his breath, his hands stretched under the car. His fingers touched the neck of the bottle he had dropped and he just managed to clutch it as he was dragged by his hair to a kneeling position. He swung blindly and felt the bottle connect with someone's hip as it broke. Billy screamed and Floyd was a little grateful he hadn't hit Tommy. His gratitude evaporated as Tommy swore and hit him across the face with a stick. Floyd felt his jaw snap as pain clawed up his face. Floyd landed back on the ground and was kicked hard in the ribs, leaving him gasping for breath as a thunderclap deafened him from overhead.

The storm tore into the area as Floyd was kicked from both sides. He stopped trying to fight back, stopped trying to cover his face from the downpour. He only tried to keep conscious, but the pain was making that hard. The beating let up even as the rain kept up.

Billy, his voice braced by pain, spat in Floyd's face.

"This lesson been sent behalf of Brother Falls. You don't want your face to be seen back in town, convict. You come back, you leave in a box"

Floyd heard them get back in the car, heard the engine rev. The car pulled into the logging road and backed out. Floyd, lying on his stomach, could see the car coming toward him and knew it would crush him. He brought together everything he had and just managed to roll over onto the grass as the wheels brushed his clothing. He could hear the sound of the motor pass him then fade in the distance. Then there was just the lightning, the rain, and the pain. Then all of that faded as well. Then all was black.

The black was all he knew now.

He tried to remember when he felt light. It was before the deluge. He still could hear his Uncle Ezekiel's voice. He must have been eight or nine then.

"Jeremiah? You finished your prayers?" His uncle's voice would be warm with love and devotion. The crash that took his parents left him untouched in the deformed origami that the family car had become after the accident. Every version that passed from one to another included the word "miracle' and the phrase "Sign from God". His uncle, pastor at the community's church, had taken him in without questions or terms. Ezekiel had more godliness in his than anyone else Jeremiah knew. Ezekiel's devotion wasn't born of the plain pine church he went to. He felt God in his marrow.

Jeremiah so wanted to know that feeling, the sense of the Lord being as near as an eyelash. All he could ever remember feeling inside was a gaping desolate void. He had accepted the feeling. Jeremiah reasoned that after all, it was his

Hours he would look at his reflection in the mirror. He always saw death's own jet black hair, hovering over dark jack rabbit eyes full of uncertainty and anxiety, his weak chin accenting his scrawny frame, and he would despair that he would be blessed.

Unknown to his uncle, Jeremiah had impure thoughts and had engaged in actions that thrilled and repulsed him with girls his age and younger. He was sure these impurities would keep him from salvation.

"How can I get God in me, Uncle? I ask every night in my prayers for His grace, for His sign. If I get Him in me I know I can preach as good as you."

Ezekiel, his bright blue eyes flashing under his sunset red hair, would wipe the hair from Jeremiah's brow and laugh like the angels.

"Child, you have the Lord in you. You spend so much time looking for Him that you let Him slide right by you. Be patient and listen to your heart and He will whisper to you when you least expect it."

Still, every night at prayers, Jeremiah asked for the faith that eluded him as easily as it found his uncle. At every service, he watched his uncle deliver sermons, many of them extemporaneous. Everyone loved the way Ezekiel preached, and they expected that Jeremiah would follow in the Pastor's footsteps. Jeremiah felt he just needed more time to absorb his uncle's teachings, his respect and dignity, his way of comforting those in need and of building confidence in people. With his uncle to guide his path, Jeremiah knew he would find his way to serve the Lord.

Ezekiel and he lived in a bachelor's world. The only woman who visited was Mizz Hannah, a widow about Ezekiel's age who came over two or three times a week to help keep the place up, whether it needed it or not. She was a very prim woman, who kept her blonde hair in a tight bun. Jeremiah at first liked her coming over. He only had to do light chores when the weather was bad. If it was nice out, he never even had to clean when she was there. Ezekiel and Hannah would encourage Jeremiah to go outside and get some fresh air and have fun while they toiled up stairs. Many times Jeremiah would come back to see the two of them sweaty and out of breath.

The incident that turned Jeremiah against Mizz Hannah occurred the day he observed one day that Mizz Hannah had something he'd never seen before – she had an hourglass figure, just like in the cartoons they showed before the movies he'd seen. He realized this one day while Mizz Hannah was standing on tip toe to dust the mantle. Entranced, he used his index fingers to follow the arcs of her body. Suddenly Mizz Hannah turned around and saw his fingers in mid-curve both fingers pointing at her Pistol-Pete style in a manner both found indecent. Her eyes, at first inquisitive, figured out what the boy was doing and her face blanched. She stormed out of the room to find Ezekiel. In the hallway he could her nasal voice beckon for the Pastor. She dragged him back into the room and informed him of Jeremiah's transgression while Ezekiel stood towering over the child. When Mizz Hannah was finished, at first Jeremiah thought he wouldn't be in any trouble because he could have sworn he saw his uncle smile. Yet when Ezekiel turned his hard stare toward Jeremiah, there was no joke there.

One April morning, after a hard spring rain, Ezekiel set out to visit Ruby Martin, who was closer to being with her Maker than most in the hollow. Going to her house meant heading down Dry Creek Run road, which most of the time was as arid as its name. Pastor Ezekiel, being a man of common sense and compassion, knew that when the rains came, you took your life in your hands when there was high water in the road. He also knew if he didn't find his way to Ruby's side, she might be alone when her end came. Eyeing the water covering the road from the main road, he figured the depth not to be more than a couple of inches. It wasn't till later that night that Jeremiah called the sheriff and a day and a half later that that Ezekiel's DeSoto was pulled out a few miles downstream.

The Pastor's funeral brought mourners from five counties, so beloved was Ezekiel. Jeremiah, now of age, was assumed by all to be the natural successor to the Pastor. Everyone praised his eloquence and the way he cared after people, the sick and helpless, and the children.

Jeremiah enrolled in the St. Louis School of Divinity, ready to take up his uncle's mantle. However, he found it increasingly hard to resolve his desire to preach God's word with his anger at God for taking his uncle. Everywhere he looked he saw teachers and students effortlessly absorbing the good word. Even though he was an excellent student, his own lack of faith made him feel impotent. He didn't quite feel right with his peers. Even though he could be sociable at mixers, he didn't quite know what do with women his age and so his awkwardness with them was the strongest social skill he developed.

In his darkness, he continued to feel his impurities ooze into actions he could not reconcile with his goals. All he could do was to push them deeper away from his awareness and forgiveness.

The one accomplishment he felt any excitement for was when he found a copy of *Malleus Malificarum*, the fifteenth century manual for dealing with suspected witches. Although it dealt with creatures Jeremiah never thought he'd ever meet, in it he found the rock hard certainty he felt he needed. There were right ways to do things, and right hard punishments if those diktats weren't followed. Everything in the book made such perfect sense to him. He finally saw why women were so alien to him. He finally saw what could be done about so that he felt safe. He didn't need to understand them; he just had to deal with them.

That it was not his uncle's standard liberated him. He had always thought his great dead uncle's one fault was his leniency. He would forgive anybody. This made the hairs on the back of Jeremiah's neck stand on end. To Jeremiah, forgiveness was a weakness, like a bad virus. Jeremiah felt that the feral pulse of emotional venom was energizing.

It was a good thing.

When he finished the book for the first time, he felt he had finally moved through his uncle's shadow. In this he was irrevocably correct.

He was the only one not surprised when he dropped out of school. His school record was strong and Jeremiah was willing to work hard. He managed a religious book store for a year, and after that at a Goodwill store in St. Louis for eighteen months. He left to work with a contractor who specialized in churches. Every place he worked at and then left found him with a good reputation and his familiar void. Even worse to him, every career choice brought him back closer to preaching.

Unable to find anything he could make a living at, unwilling to live with his gifts or demons, he came back to the one calling he could not turn away from. If he could not control his drives, he could at least control the flocks that turned toward him for guidance. As the years went on, the further into his soul Falls pushed his darkness, the harder his darkness pushed back.

It was a quiet ride back through the downpour for the brothers in the dark. Tommy drove while Billy tended to his hip, pulling shards of glass from his jeans. After a long silence, Billy yelped as he pulled a thick piece of bottle from his hip and turned to talk to Billy.

"Damn that Craiven. Damn near smashed my hip. Might've crippled me."

"Aww, stop yer damn whining. He just give back some of whut you give him."

"You feelin' sorry for that summbitch, Tommy? Wanna go back and carry him to a doctor?"

"That ain't what we signed on for, ain't what we agreed to. Brother wanted Floyd to get what he didn't get from the courts."

"And it'll be God's way if'n he don't make it out of them woods. Any luck, if the beatin' don't take him, exposure will."

Just outside of the town limits, Billy pulled into a gas station, closed for the night. A long black Ford Marquis sat by the pumps, its motor running, its headlights off. Billy nosed up window to window so that he could address the driver. The automatic window purred down. Falls leaned out.

"How'd it go, boys?"

"Billy got a little hurt."

"You all right, boy?"

Billy leaned forward and gritted.

"Yessir – nothing a little rest won't cure."

Tommy could see Falls' eyes gleam in the darkness. Something about them gave him the willies.

"You a good boy, Billy. You too, Tommy. I might have more of the Lord's work for you."

Tommy felt a growing suspicion.

"What kind of work?"

Billy was more eager.

"What kind of money?"

"Same as you got for this. We've got another partner of Satan to lead back to God's path."

Tommy felt suspicion well up like heartburn.

"Who?"

Fells paused. He had no trouble so far in convincing the brothers to do his bidding on behalf of the Lord. Yet there was a tone in Tommy's voice that told Falls he might be pushing too far too fast with him, at least. For now, he addressed his reply to Billy.

"Old woman Sonoria."

Tommy spoke up.

"What's she done?"

"Don't matter. If Brother Falls says she's gone down the left hand path, that's good enough for me. Ya want her spooked or worse?"

"She needs to see that her witching ways hurt the community." Falls voice sounded a little distant, even though he sat only a few feet away.

Tommy started to argue until he saw the bright rabid look in Billy's eyes. No use arguing with Billy, much less trying to get him to even acknowledge anyone else was there. Best he could do was to go with Billy to keep him from going too far over a line he wasn't sure Billy hadn't already crossed.

"She'll be tough to track down. I caint think of anyone knows where her cabin is." Billy said, thinking.

Tommy, watching Billy think, watching his eyes blaze with malevolence, found a seed of sureness in his heart.

"This'll be the last time we serve you, Brother." Tommy said with conviction.

Brother Falls drove home, clear and comfortable that Floyd had suffered the Lord's will through his dispensation. After soaking in near scalding water with drops of rose and High John the Conqueror's oil to cleanse his body and spirit, he dressed in a smoking jacket and pajama bottoms. He ate a simple meal of soup and toast and then lit a fire in the fireplace.

He sat on a bench in front of the fireplace watching the flames, becoming lost in the colors and swirls of red and blue; becoming lost in the brandy and the void.

He knew these people in this town. But he had never known anyone like Aradia Sonoria. She didn't even need church to know her faith. She grasped wisdom that Falls couldn't even sense. It terrified him, the knowledge that there was lore that couldn't be constrained, couldn't be classified, fundamental essences that could be gained only through dedication. What infuriated him was that he couldn't dominate people with that faculty. If he couldn't manipulate them, well, he could at least show them the error of their ways. The way he would show old woman Sonoria what he was capable of.

He stood and looked over his bookshelves, which covered an entire wall from ceiling to floor before sitting down in his recliner with a snifter of brandy and a copy of the Malificarum. Focusing on Question Six in the manual *'Why is it that Women are chiefly addicted to Evil superstitions?'* Falls read how the Inquisition's irrefutable truths dealt with women who refused to honor what Falls knew to be God's ways. He fell asleep with the book in his hands, dreaming warm dreams of old woman Sonoria burning at a stake.

It was in the middle of the night that Falls woke up in a cold sweat, barely remembering the tiny accusing fingers pointing at him. He made a mental note to take of that later in the day.

Floyd's tremors woke him up. The light, as dim as it was, hurt. Everything hurt. Floyd wanted to cry but that hurt even worse. The rain had stopped. Floyd lay on his back and tried to assess his condition. He could breathe through his pain. He hoped that meant that his ribs hadn't pierced one of his lungs. When he tried opening his mouth the pain made tears come to his eyes.

He smelled of rain and vomit, though thankfully the downpour had rinsed most of the retch off. He couldn't stay where he was – anything, anyone could do him harm. He looked to his right and left. A few feet away, in the grass on his right side, he could see the branch he had used to steady himself.

He reached out and grabbed the turf with his hand and began pulling himself slowly. He had to stop every few inches and pause until the dizziness of his aching subsided. As he neared the limb, he began to notice through the red haze of hurt the logging road. He wondered if it led anywhere. He knew his daddy used to come up this road running moonshine when the loggers were still here, knew that there used to be shanties. His hope fueling his strength, he managed to reach the limb, managed to leverage his body to a kneeling, then to a standing position. He no longer trembled with chill. The exertion it took to get this far left him steaming in the morning dew, his body hot from soreness.

Using his free hand, he squeezed his shirt sleeve and ran the wetness over his face. Even though the smell of his sour mucus, sweat and blood made him queasy, it still felt good and gave him the energy to hobble to the logging road.

He made his way down the road slowly, taking time every few minutes to lean against a tree to catch his equilibrium. Hours passed to Floyd, though he thought it odd the sun didn't move all that much. Floyd stopped to rest and looked down. A path, not much more than a scratch, went off to his left. Looking up, through the trees, Floyd thought he saw some sort of structure in the distance. Girding his diminishing energy, he hauled his throbbing body through the underbrush.

As he neared he saw what it was – a simple one room pine plank house, falling apart from abandonment. With an unexpected pang of self-pity, Floyd knew what that home felt like to be rejected and derelict.

As he neared, Floyd felt his exhaustion grow. With any luck, there would be a place he could lay down for a while and rest. He didn't fool himself that there would be food left in the place. Not that he would eat anything if there was food. Though his hunger was growing, he didn't want to risk screwing up his jaw any more than it might be already.

The porch bent and groaned as he stepped on it. The supports for the roof were trunks that still had bark on them. He looked up to see the porch roof sagging in the middle. It didn't look like this place had too many more seasons in her. Floyd looked down and could see the ground through the numerous holes in the floorboards where chunks of the woods had rotted. He kept a mind to watch where he stepped; no use to add a broken leg to his other injuries.

Inside there were two rooms – the main room and a room off to the left. The main room was empty except the dirt and leaves that covered the floors. The walls once had been painted with a flat white paint; the sheen had left with the house's memory of its residents. There were lighter squares and rectangles along one side of the wall where sinks and appliances had once been attached, and holes for pipes and wiring. The windows had long been stripped of whatever panes they had and the breeze moved the leaves unfettered across the floor.

The other room had seen some occupation – there was a twin size cot mattress inside a cedar wood frame on the floor. There was a closet catty corner from the bed, its door shut. Floyd tried the door. It wouldn't budge. Stuck shut, he supposed. A piece of 2x4 had been nailed to the wall secured the bed frame. Ropes were attached to it. Another piece of wood lay nailed to the floor at the foot of the frame; ropes were attached there as well. A couple of torn scraps of clothing lay on the floor. Just below the scraps were dark stains.

Floyd looked carefully at the clothing. It was sky blue, with a stars and quarter moon motif. The patterns on the cloth were more childlike than adult, and it left Floyd with an uneasy feeling. He remembered Dawkins describing what the Cunningham girl was wearing when she disappeared.

Floyd had never been one to put himself in anyone's business, and was not used to the pangs of conscience he was feeling. For a few moments his pain and hunger subsided as he tried to assess and resolve these new and unwelcome emotions. The words he said to that little girl's mother came back to maul him worse than any pain he was feeling.

The sound of a car in the distance made him look up with a start. He thought it might be the brothers come back to give him more of the same. He hobbled back the way he came. Standing on the porch, Floyd looked for a hiding spot as the car's roar neared, then stopped. He could hear a car door open and shut. There was nowhere to go. He looked down. He might be able to get under the porch. Bracing against the corner of the house, he lowered to the ground with a painful groan and slid under the porch, leaving his branch lying against the edge of the porch. It was painfully hard for him to breathe lying in that position. Overriding this worrisome soreness was his reluctance to risk another beating by whoever it was approaching. Floyd was not risking the attempt to readjust to a more comfortable position, and doubted he could find one.

He could hear leaves crunch underfoot and come closer. He couldn't see the upper torso of the approaching person, though he could see his crisply pressed black trousers and his shiny black shoes. As the shoes stepped on the porch, Floyd squeezed out of sight as best he could under the holes in the porch.

'It might be a trooper', Floyd worried. The footsteps went into the house. Floyd figured whoever it was went into the back room. After a moment, the sound of the footsteps came back. They clunked back onto the porch and stepped off. Floyd saw the shoes walk toward the trees. Thirty yards or so away from the house, he stopped.

He could now see enough of the man's upper torso to see the shovel in his right hand. He held his left hand to his midsection, as if holding something. Floyd could not see his face because of the hat the man wore. He stopped and dropped the thing he held in his left hand. Floyd still could not tell what he was concealing.

His back to Floyd, he began digging by a tree. Floyd could see the effort he put into it, the sense of urgency. Floyd wondered why the man seemed like a peeping tom about to be discovered by the owner of the house, here in the middle of nowhere.

Furtively, the man pushed the dirt into the hole with his shoe and covered the cavity back up, using the shovel to scatter some leaves over and around the excavation. When he finished, it was hard to tell that any digging had taken place. He stood there for a moment, breathing hard. Floyd figured that he wasn't a working man. Then he turned and faced Floyd. It was Brother Falls. Falls began retracing his steps toward his car. Floyd heard the car door open and shut, and then heard the car turn over and drive off, its engine humming off into the distance.

He pulled himself out from under the porch with a grunting effort and paused, breathing heavy and painfully. His jaw pulsed with hurt. Using the corner of the house he eased himself up and grabbed the branch just as he began to lose his balance. Curiosity out weighing exhaustion, he made his way to the tree and cleared away the soil with his branch while he leaned against the tree. After a few seconds of turning, some sky blue cloth was unearthed, its stars obscured by dirt. Floyd wondered why there was only one piece of the cloth there. He was sure he'd seen two or three pieces on the floor. Floyd concealed the cloth again.

Although Floyd was never brought up to have any great respect for figures of the community, he still, in the small of his heart, wanted to think that some of them could be trusted. He tasted the familiar bitterness of being let down thinking about it.

Suddenly and unexpectedly the exertion caught up with Floyd. He doubled over with pain and hunger. He knew he had to find some shelter as surely as he knew he couldn't stay at that house. If anyone found him there he'd see a needle in his arm before he saw another day of freedom. Slowly he made his way back to the road. He figured his best hope was to follow the road and hope that he'd find somewhere to rest, maybe find a garden to take something from.

With a last dejected look for refuge he knew he wouldn't find, he trudged off parallel to the road headed back toward town, far enough into the brush that he wasn't easily seen from the road, yet close enough to keep his eye on the rutted brown ribbon of road. With increasing regularity, Floyd had to stop to catch his breath or to lean against a tree and rest his done in legs or to pull out burrs that poked through his pants and scratched his legs or to pull off ticks trying to get fastened into his skin.

Late in the afternoon, after seeing no cars and no buildings, Floyd saw a trail feeding off into the deeper woods. It wasn't much, a passage into what may have been nowhere. Floyd thought maybe he might find a cabin or some backwoods lodge hunters used during the season. His energy diminishing with every step, Floyd followed the road.

Once he had lost sight of the main road, such as it was, the sun which had at least warmed him, vanished behind towers of dark cumulus clouds. Floyd began to shiver and his legs were beginning to throb painfully. There was nowhere to go but forward. Floyd swallowed his discomfort and continued into the dusk. A loud rumble from the storm clouds moving in inspired Floyd to try move quicker, but his body no longer readily obeyed him. The tremors increased with the hard winds bringing in the thunderstorm. He walked into the dusk.

Then the rains came. The winds blowing so hard it rained sideways. Floyd walked on, getting wetter and sicker by the minute. The gale howled so it grated his bones with every step. He didn't even notice when the road meandered away into underbrush.

Floyd began to think he could see a figure in the forest ahead of him. Never in plain view, Floyd could see a small person aways off. Floyd thought the mystery person looked like a kid or a circus midget. He could see them darting in and out between the trees. He began to follow whoever it might be, his energy quickly ebbing.

"You got to slow up some – I caint follow that fast." Floyd said to the deep woodland. Floyd had to pause every few seconds to wipe his eyes clear from the downpour. Meanwhile, ahead of his vision, the figure continued on.

"Help me find my way." He pleaded to the dark green surrounding him...

Floyd tripped over a vine root and fell hard to his knees and then his stomach. He dropped his only support, the branch. He never noticed his wallet slipping out of his pocket. He continued on, driven by sheer willpower, on his hands and knees, his palms slipping in the wet leaves. He tried to call for whoever had been leading him, but they were gone.

He crawled out of the forest into a clearing, his tremors getting worse by the second. He had no real idea where he was, or that he had left the woods. He reached a fence with a furrow beyond it as his arms gave way and he lay there on his stomach, with nothing but the void to greet him.

It might have been a child's laugh or a crow's caw, Aradia thought as she woke from her dozing. She roused herself with the barren realization that, what ever it was she heard, it was still the present. She listened to the downpour on the roof and canopies.

"I used to love the rain", she said to the empty room.

She used to love many things. Rubbing her face in an attempt to stop moping, she rose and went to heat some water for tea. Glancing out the window as she passed she saw something at the edge of the garden

"Too big for a bobcat; too small for a bear."

She thought it might be a coyote, but it didn't look right.

She pulled on her boots and threw a slicker over her shoulder and went into the dusk to see. She grabbed the pitchfork from its hook on the wall on her way out, just in case the critter was stubborn.

It was hard to see through the rain. It wasn't until she was a few yards away from the figure when she realized it was human. She reached the body and cautiously turned it over. His face was a mass of bruises and his jaw was swelling badly. The man was trembling as if in seizure.

Aradia put the pitchfork down and grabbed the man under the armpits and pulled him back to the cabin. Even though there was a chill in the air, he was so hot she could see steam coming off his head.

Inside, she left him by the heat of the Franklin stove while she set up a cot for him. She brought a pan of warm soapy water over and washed him as she stripped him down. She gasped when she saw his upper torso, covered with wavy quilts of purple and red. She de-ticked him, putting the ticks into a bottle of rubbing alcohol as she went over his body.

Bruised as he was, she couldn't recognize him. She never went into town much, so she thought the odds were that she wouldn't know him anyway.

She wrapped him in wool blankets and a quilt. His tremors kept up unabated. With a physical therapist's assurance, she reset his dislocated jaw with a snap. The patient never even noticed.

She went into the kitchen and opened up her herb closet, picking some ginseng root, some rose hips, and some garlic. She seeped the rose hips in hot water and mashed the ginseng and garlic into a paste, which she transferred into a bowl. She took a turkey baster from a drawer and went back out to administer to her patient. Using the baster, she fed him the tea and paste until the bowl was empty. She adjusted his blankets and fed the fire before sitting down with a book. Every so often she would wipe his face with a cloth to cool him down.

She wondered what she would do if he died during the night.

Dawkins was finishing up the weekly arrest report that would be sent to the newspaper when the knock resonated through the door. Pullman entered, wheezing from the walk up two flights from his office to Dawkins' office. He only walked up when Dawkins asked to see him personally.

"You left a message with Margaret that you needed to see me when I got out of court?" The way Pullman made it sound, Dawkins thought, you would've thought that Pullman was being asked to skin his youngest child rather than pay a courtesy call. Pullman didn't like to leave his office except in case of a state emergency or a free buffet.

"I got a call from Johnny McGavock about an hour ago. Seems Floyd Craiven's turned up missing. Gone three days now."

"Why is that our problem? It's not like we got a warrant for him. He ain't jumped bail. Let McGavock file a missing person's report."

"Oh, he did. Thing is, couple of my boys took Craiven to the Alibi Motel over on 28. Least, that's what they told me when I asked them."

"Why'd you figure to use county man hours on escorting a piece of horse shit like Craiven anywhere?"

"Brother Falls had a mob of folks outside the jail. You musta heard them hollering. I was ready to take him somewhere myself until the Boarson boys offered to take him out of the city limits. When I asked where they went, Billy Boarson said Floyd wanted to go to the Alibi. Said they dropped him off there and that was the last they saw of him. Talked to Crystal over there and she said he never came in to get a room."

"Craiven's a big boy. We got problems of our own. Proving he killed Lila Cunningham, for example."

"Yeah, well, we've been over his place and his car here and back again. Had the state boys out and a team of forensic scientists from the F.B.I. and all they found was dirty dishes and dirty books. We can't put her with him at any time and for all I know, those panties in his car were to check the oil, like he said."

"Then why didn't he say so when he was stopped?'

"Floyd ain't ever been the sharpest blade in the box cutter. I think all that time he spent in JD and the road crews might have sweetened him to life on the inside. That's just my view, though. Might be wrong."

"Craiven and his people have been a thorn in this community going back three generations. He needs to be made an example of."

"Only if he breaks the law."

"Unless we stop him before he breaks the law."

"You develop some second sight I didn't know about? Purd, we known each other most of our lives. Grown up with most of the folks in this town. How many of them would break a serious law if they thought they'd get away with it? More than you might think, I guarantee. We gonna arrest all of them because of what they'd like to do?"

"Most of the folks in town aren't like the Craivens. They don't wanna be like the Craivens. We got a right to keep the Craivens from poisoning innocent minds."

"I ain't got any deep love for the Craivens, or for Floyd, but you can't argue they had more than their share of bad breaks and nasty whispers from church going folks like you and me. Every man deserves redemption on his own terms."

"You go on thinking that, Doug Dawkins, and you'll find yourself turned out by every sob story and hustler from one side of the state line to the other."

"I'm clear on my job. Step in once a law's been broken and catch the perpetrator."

"And I'm clear on mine. Protect the community from bad influences, no matter."

Falls felt it deep. The pressure inside that just kept building. He could no longer reason with it.

"I'm churning inside just like everyone else; trying to carry the charge of the Lord." he told himself out loud, though his words did little to quiet the agitation within.

He wasn't sure of the reason for his distress. He tried praying, he'd tried fasting. He'd even tried flagellation, something he hadn't thought necessary since St. Louis.

His growing impatience was not helped by his meeting with Billy. It had been Billy's idea to meet without Tommy there. They got together in the lot by the ball fields.

"Have you found old woman Sonoria?"

"We havin' problems. She don't go to town but once in a blue moon. She grows her own food and she don't have a phone. I talked to Johnny over at the post office. She gets her mail delivered to a post box. Comes in every once in a while to get it, or her girl Diane gets it for her."

"We need that woman found. Time runs short for idlers." Falls venomous tones surprised him and unsettled Billy.

"Don't get mad at me, Brother. I'm trying my best. Only so much one man can do. Tommy don't show interest in this."

"Billy – you're a good shepard of the Lord. I know you'll find a way to track that witch down. You'll do it for your own salvation if nothing else."

Falls felt a little better seeing the fear grow in Billy's eyes. Though within his soul, Falls' knew that his feelings of comfort would be short-lived. Then the pressure would come back.

Floyd had been having a lifetime of strange dreams. Forests that walked and talked. Cats and birds that would become human then turn back into animal form. Breezes whispered things he knew to be very old truths that he would then forget as soon as heard them. Dancing lights around mushroom rings. Every so often he would taste something warm and earthy sour in his mouth and feel better shortly afterwards.

He felt his hand fall from his chest and strike something round and plastic. He turned his stiff neck to one side and saw a bedpan on the floor. He looked up and saw a rough hewn log ceiling. He wasn't wet, or hungry. Through a window he could see blue sky.

He wasn't in a hospital. He didn't think he was dead. If he had been deceased, he would not have expected the kind of environment he was in

"Back to the land of the living, are we?"

At first it was just a disembodied voice, and then he saw the woman walk in from the other room. She seemed tall to Floyd, until he realized that it was the way she carried herself. She was confident. She moved smoothly, like a dancer. She looked to be about fifty, as near as Floyd could figure, even though Floyd was the first to admit he was not very good at guessing someone's age. Her hair was more silver than black, though she still had a fair amount of black in her hair. Her face was more oblong than oval, with very little wrinkling. Her eyes looked silver in some sunshine and blue when she stood a different way in the light. She had a warm smile, although she made Floyd feel like she knew more than she was telling.

Floyd tried to rise up on an elbow; the effort was like lifting a motor onto an A-frame with his bare hands. He managed enough to get a look at the room where he lay.

The room that housed Floyd was large and well lit. There were windows on three walls and a skylight to bring in more sun for the plants directly underneath it. Besides the cot and Franklin stove, there weren't a lot of furnishings. A couple of rocking chairs book ending a table and lamp, an old couch and the table for the plants. On the table was a fish tank with a couple of goldfish. One side of the wall had a table with a knife, a glass, some candles and an incense burner. On the wall behind it was a quilt with some sort of swirl pattern.

"Where am I?" He was surprised to find it hardly hurt when he talked.

"I found you at the edge of my property. You looked about half past dead. You've slept four days straight since then. My name's Aradia Sonoria. What's your name?"

Floyd paused, his heart beginning to beat fast. He could hardly tell her who he was, given the circumstances.

"I'm – Earl. Earl White. I thank you for your kindness. Maybe I should head on out though."

He tried to get up, until his body put up an argument he couldn't counter. He fell back onto the cot.

"You aren't going anywhere yet, Earl. I don't get much company anymore out here. How'd you end up this far out of town in the shape you were in?"

Floyd thought quickly.

"Met a couple of fellas in a bar. They got me drunk, brought me out to some road, beat me and left me for the coyotes."

"That explains why you didn't have any wallet in your clothes."

Floyd instinctively felt for his wallet. It was only then he realized he was naked under the sheet.

"Where are my clothes?"

"Hanging up in the clothes. Washed them for you."

"I'll thank you for that too, Mrs. Sonoria.

"You call me Aradia. You need a couple more days rest. Then you can head out for the sheriff and tell him about your misfortune. Don't have a phone here, sorry to say. My daughter's been into me to get one. Don't have that many folks I wanna call."

She smiled and Floyd felt safe. He yawned.

"You need rest. When you wake up we'll get some food in you."

Dawkins was enjoying the first warm air of spring. The window was open wide and Dawkins was watching a large Pilated Woodpecker hunting for bugs in the tree a few feet from his window. He wished he'd had a camera in the office to take a picture for Aaron, his grandson, who was in the habit of imitating Woody Woodpecker. He was still smiling when Tommy Boarson stood and knocked on the open door.

"Morning, Tom. Beautiful day out there. Maybe get some fishing in later. You up for it?"

Dawkins thought Tommy looked a little lost. Tommy looked down either side of the corridor and came into the office, closing the door behind him.

"Sheriff, I got something I need to git off m'chest. You got a minute?"

Dawkins motioned for him to take a seat and leaned back in his chair.

"What's botherin' you, Tom?"

"There ain't no easy way to put this Sheriff, because I let you down."

"What you talkin' 'bout?"

"The other day, when you asked me 'bout takin' Floyd to the Alibi, it was a lie I told you an' I'm sorry."

"How was it a lie?"

Dawkins felt a growing unease within him. He wasn't sure where this was going; he was only certain he wouldn't like it.

"Billy and I took him down one of the old logging roads. We wanted to teach him a lesson, was all. Gave him a licking and left him there. I ain't been to sleep over it, since I heard Floyd disappeared. Somethin's bad come to him, I fear."

"Whose notion was it to give him the licking?"

Tommy paused for enough of a second for Dawkins to know he was going to lie.

"It were all me, sir. Billy didn't have nothing to do with it. I'll give up my job if that's what you want."

Dawkins turned toward the window and scratched his nose, thinking for a moment. He turned back to Tommy, sitting ramrod straight in the chair.

"Tommy, how long we known each other?"

"I known you and your folks since I was old enough to crawl, I s'ppose."

"Right. I known you and Billy a long time. I know what kind of man you are and what kind Billy is. Truth be told, I never would've taken Billy on in this office unless you were gonna come with him. Billy's got the mean streak and you got the reasonable one. I figured you to keep Billy from goin' over th' line. You would never do somethin' like this unless someone prodded you – someone who you might respect or 'least abide by. It weren't me and the only other feller you ever talk of with any level of reverence is Brother Falls. You tell me true now – did he put you all up to this?"

Tommy looked away and shook his head.

"It was me – all me, like I done told."

Dawkins took on his harshest tone, the one he used on real hard cases.

"Boy, you might be in a world of trouble here. You got to get straight with me and first and more important you got to get straight with yourself. I know you're tryin' to lie to protect Billy and maybe Falls and you're doin' a piss poor job with it. You let me know now; did the Brother put you boys up to this?"

Misery flooded Tommy's eyes and he nodded, looking down to the floor in shame. Dawkins got up and moved to Tommy, putting his hand on the boys trembling shoulder.

"Tom, you done a man's deed comin' in to tell me this. Does Billy know you were comin' to talk to me?"

Tommy, still unable to speak a full sentence, shook his head. Dawkins took a quick glance at the work schedule.

"He ain't due in till tonight. All right, then. You and me gonna take a ride out to where you all left Floyd."

Falls sat in his car in front of the post office, going through the junk mail he'd gotten from his mailbox. He looked up to see Diane Cunningham, daughter of the witch Sonoria, go into the post office. He picked up his cell phone and dialed a number. Billy answered, his voice full of sleep and sand.

"What you want?"

"Billy, its Brother Falls. Old woman Sonoria's daughter just walked into the post office. I'll bet she's on her way back to her momma's cabin when she gets out. Are you ready to do God's work?"

There was a pause on the line.

"I imagine. If you leave now and get me, we can pick up her trail as she leaves the town limits."

"I'm on my way."

Falls felt the righteousness of the day burn in him bright as an inquisition as he started up his car.

Floyd awoke early the next morning to find Aradia sitting next to him in a rocker, reading a book. Floyd looked at the front cover. 'Poems by Rumi'. The name didn't sound familiar.

"Some alky wrote a book?"

Aradia laughed in the way a songbird might greet the day.

"No, no. Rumi was a famous Persian poet in the thirteenth century. He wrote wonderful verse. Would you like to read something?"

"Well, I ain't never been much of a reader, but I'll take a gander. Don't expect me to make head nor tail of it though."

"Fair enough."

Aradia closed the book and handed it to him. Floyd took the book and opened it. The poem on the page seemed to leap out at him. The title was 'The Guest House'

This being human is a guest house.

Every morning a new arrival.

A joy, a depression, a meanness,
some momentary awareness comes
as an unexpected visitor.

Welcome and entertain them all!

Even if they're a crowd of sorrows,
who violently sweep your house
empty of its furniture,
still, treat each guest honorably.

He may be clearing you out
for some new delight.

The dark thought, the shame, the malice,
meet them at the door laughing,
and invite them in.

Be grateful for whoever comes,
because each has been sent
as a guide from beyond.

THE GUEST HOUSE"
by Jelaluddin Balkhi Rumi (1207-1248), translated by Coleman Barks

Floyd lay the book on his chest and thought about what he'd read.

"This feller lived eight hundred years ago, you said?"

Aradia nodded.

"I right don't know what to make of it. It kinda makes sense to me, though I cain't put my finger on it."

"Well, don't try to force anything, Let it come to you as it comes. Are you hungry?"

Floyd ate the soup and fresh herb bread Aradia made with the poem nagging at him.

'Let in shame and sorrows?' he thought to himself

"You ever been so ashamed of yourself you couldn't face it?" Floyd asked Aradia quietly. She looked at him wryly from across the table.

"I've done a lot of things I'm not proud of, Earl. Had a baby before I was probably ready to do so. Married a man for safety and not love, and then took my anger out on him unfairly for doing so."

"What about bein' a witch?" Floyd wished he could have bitten the words off before he said them.

"Who said I was a witch?"

"Well – I done heard things around town. You know."

"Does it bother you that people say I'm a witch?"

Floyd shrugged his shoulders.

"Don't rightly know. Ain't me they're sayin' it about."

"You ever go to church, Earl?"

A scornful look flew across Floyd's eyes.

""I figure there's enough hypo-crassy in this world without me takin' my time to listen to words that a preacher don't really believe in and that don't ring true to me. Ain't never had use for fire and brimstone. Seen too much of hell here to worry 'bout a heaven somewhere else that might or might not be there for me when it's my time."

"What about faith?"

"What about it? Just a word to me."

"Faith is what makes spirituality breathes, not a bible, or a torah, or a Koran or a Veda. Men can make words jump through hoops; faith can make man walk through fire and come through unscathed. Maybe I'm not a witch. Maybe I just want to worship God in my own way and by what or who I name the Creator. Maybe my faith means for me that I find my faith through my work, and through the earth, through the way I understand the voices in the wind and the secrets in the land. Sometimes faith is just watching the world and what's in it as if it were a painting – a still life, if you like."

Aradia paused for a moment.

"You know, some say that those they call witches follow the old way, the foundation for Christianity as most know it. They were the healers, the midwives long ago."

Floyd shook his head and frowned.

"Sounds a bunch of mumbo jumbo you ask me. No offense, ma'am, just the way it seems to me."

"Oh, I've heard worse. I don't ask anyone to accept my way of worship if they don't ring true to them."

"That's a sight better than any pastor I ever heard spout. Lest you give a feller ways to bow out if'n it don't feel right."

"That's how all religion should be, don't you think? Otherwise, it's nothing more than boxed goods you buy on a shelf. That poem you read is about faith, in a way. Faith in knowing yourself – in accepting the shadows."

"Whut the hell you talkin' 'bout – shadows?"

Aradia smiled.

"We go through our days choosing to face the dark corners in us or not. You've learned to live your life based on other's worse expectations of you."

"How can you know that?"

"Earl, I know people. I'm pretty sure that there are things you haven't told me about yourself. I have a feeling your name isn't Earl – it doesn't fit you for some reason."

"Then why do you let me stay?"

"Because there is light in you. Light I don't think you really see. Light that hasn't been acknowledged by others. I know what a closed town this is. I hear what people whisper about me behind my back. That's one reason I decided to move out to the backwoods."

She paused for Floyd to answer. Seeing that he was thinking over what she'd said, she continued.

"We live with our shadows or we run from them. But we can't ever really hide; we become like them in order to evade their radar, or we become so rigid in thinking we have avoided them that we become worse than even we might have thought possible. Or we face them and move on with our lives and our potential. The kind of potential I see in you, Earl - the potential to do great things for people."

Floyd felt that same uncomfortable welling of conscience that he felt that day at the cabin.

"Aradia, you been good to me. You do what you need to when I tell you this; I won't blame you or think the worse of you for it. My name ain't Earl. I'm Floyd Craiven."

He watched her for a response. She remained composed, except for the color that touched her cheeks.

"I wanna tell you now – I didn't do harm to your granddaughter."

"I believe you, Earl – I mean, Floyd." Her voice was now very small.

"Part of what I told you were right. After I left court last week, I was taken out to an old logging road and beaten on the word of Brother Falls. When I come to, I made my way to a cabin where I saw Falls bury some blue cloth with stars and moons on it. I can show you the tree where he put it. It was a stone's throw from the porch where I scooted under."

At this Aradia blanched and put her hand to her mouth. Tears began to well up in her eyes. She stood up and went to stare out the window, her back toward Floyd.

"You found that at a run down cabin."

From her tone, he wasn't sure if Aradia was asking a question or making a statement. He felt that he had to say something.

"Yes'm."

Floyd sensed the woods suddenly go still. Aradia put her hand on a pane of glass and rested her head there.

Lila's favorite skirt was made of that fabric. You didn't see any sign of her?"

Floyd shook his head.

"Naught a sign."

Aradia was quiet.

"How are you feeling?"

"Right enough, I suppose."

"Can you find it again? The cabin"

"If we can make it back to the loggin' road, I believe I can make way to it."

"You get some clothes on and take me there, please."

Standing on the porch, Floyd felt a little woozy, though he knew it'd pass soon. He stepped into the yard and got his first good look at the place. The original place must've been a century old – maybe more. Floyd recognized the rock foundation as the type you only saw in really old houses. The exterior walls had been kept nice and replaced when necessary. The roof was in slightly worse shape. There were a few patches where shingles had blown off two and three at a spot. Floyd was grateful there was something he could. He wasn't sure he'd like feeling beholden to someone, but he thought he'd give a try and see how it felt.

Hedges of butterfly bushes arced around the yard on either side. A marlin house stood high in the side yard. Beyond that was a fenced in area that contained a black wood frame about six square feet. It was filled with sand, raked into circular and swirly patterns around five large river rocks placed here and there. Aradia stepped onto the porch and joined Floyd.

"What's that?" asked Floyd, pointing to the fenced area.

"That's my Zen garden."

"What's that?"

"It's a place I go when I want everything to be very serene."

"Ya mean like – what – some sort of hidin' place?"

Floyd could have sworn he saw a flicker of a smile light her face.

"Well, more like a sanctuary, though I've done my share of hiding in there."

They turned and crossed toward the other side of the house. Floyd was impressed by the size and layout

"It was wrong of me to lie to you and I apologize. I just need you to believe me when I say what happened to your girl wasn't any of my doing."

Aradia looked away for a moment, then breathed deeply, then looked back to Floyd and looked deep into his eyes. Floyd felt her probing into his soul through his eyes, knew somehow there was no place to hide from her steady gaze. He couldn't even turn away. Abruptly Aradia nodded and spoke.

"I appreciate finding this out from you instead of someone else. I have to get you to Sheriff Dawkins."

"For what? Was two of his deputies – the Boarson boys – beat me. Don't know that he ain't involved hisself. Falls got a mighty long reach round here."

Aradia smiled ruefully.

"I know that all too well. There are a lot of people who prefer not to look within themselves – who prefer not to face the fear and anger that hide in their shadows. They're the perfect flock for someone who feeds them fearfulness – of the unknown, circumstances out of the usual run of things."

Floyd considered this and nodded.

"I seen folks rather wear blinders than face that things ain't always easy to figure. Some things don't cubbyhole even when you want 'em to – especially feelings, I reckon."

"Perhaps that's what that poem's about, Floyd. About standing up to feelings that aren't familiar to us."

"Maybe so."

Diane was driving from instinct alone; she could not get her mind off of Lila. Her rational mind still hoped she was alive somewhere. She had sat up night after bleak night, scrying into the black waters of her bowl and sensing into every emotional crevice she knew Lila to have. Everywhere she looked, a blank tone was found. Her Sight told her that Lila had crossed into Summerland, beyond the harm of whoever had hurt her. For that, she was thankful. There was so little about this nightmare to be grateful for. Dawkins and Pullman had let her down, talking out of the side of their mouths as they explained how that man had walked free. Yet, something bothered her about Craiven.

When she had scanned him, something didn't feel right. She didn't sense Lila around him, the way she would be if he had been the last person with her. Maybe he had an accomplice with him and he did the – she couldn't bring herself to say that word even mentally. She wasn't ready. She had moved into her mother's old house in town for Lila's sake, so her daughter would have playmates nearby. Now she could hardly breathe in the house. Maybe she should take her mother's suggestion and stay at her cabin for a few days, a few weeks, longer. Her mother would know what to do.

Falls and Billy followed Diane by the dust trail her Honda left. There were no off roads, so they had no worries about losing her.

"When we get there, Billy, you know what do with the witch?"

"I figure to just scare her – get her to leave town."

"And if it takes more?"

"What more you want done?"

"You may have to sacrifice the witch and the daughter."

"That's a whole lot more than I was thinkin' 'bout."

"Billy, you know what that good book says –'Suffer not a witch to live.'"

Billy was quiet for a few moments.

"Where you gonna be?"

"I'll stay by the car in case she slips past you."

"I'd druther you come along, in case I need your fortitude. I ain't got a lot of experience doin' away with women, witches or not."

Falls considered this. It might benefit the boy for him to see first hand Falls' own dedication to God's works. And if Billy ever proved unreliable, it would be something to motivate Billy to move on. Or whatever the situation might call for. Falls was a pragmatic man.

Floyd and Aradia ate lunch in silence. Floyd kept wanting to say more – that he was sorry, that he would take care of Falls, that he would mend his ways. Floyd had never been much for words, or had use for them – they were something to get his way, by guile or intimidation. Now, for once, he wanted them to mean something and all he could do was sit there like a goose laying a brick.

For her part, Aradia sat picking at her salad, weeding it more than eating. She wouldn't say so to Floyd, but she was doubtful that she could get Dawkins to listen to the very man who had been charged with the same crime that he now was accusing a leader of the community of being involved with. She believed Floyd, though she was dubious that her support would mean more than a hill of beans. Suddenly a wave of despondency overcame her. Falls would never be charged with the death of Lila. She had nowhere to go but where she was. She could not stay in this place if there was no justice, though. The sound of a car in the distance brought her back to reality.

"That sounds like Diane's car. I don't particularly want to explain your being here right now. Would you mind going in the back room while I talk with her?"

"That sounds like a fine idea, Aradia."

Diane picked up the mail and a bag of groceries she had bought for her mother and started down the path to the cabin. She thought she could hear a car down the road, though thought little of it. Kids were always using the road for a lovers lane. Few if any could follow the path from the road to the cabin. Aradia was waiting for her as she came into the clearing where the cabin sat. Aradia seemed a little out of sorts, though given everything that had happened, that didn't seem so unusual.

"Hello, Diane. How are you, honey?"

"Okay, mom. Are you all right?"

"As well as can be, I guess. Anything new in the mail?"

Diane looked over the stack in her hand.

"Dunno. I'll bring this in and we can see."

Aradia glanced toward the cabin, which Diane thought was a little odd. She had walked up on the porch when she noticed that Aradia was now looking beyond her, down the path. Diane turned around and saw Brother Falls and one of the deputies walking toward them. The hairs stood up on the back of Diane's neck, though she didn't understand why. She looked back to Aradia to see her mother as white as ice. Diane turned to stand side by side with her mother. Something was wrong, and though she didn't know what it was, they would face it together.

"Afternoon." Billy said. There was no friendliness in his voice. "We come to see you all off."

"What are you talking about?" Diane replied, a wisp of uncertainty in her voice.

"We're simple folk here and we don't cotton to your witch's ways." Falls stated.

"Who do you think you are?" Aradia demanded.

"We're God's soldiers, sent to remove you one way or the other from this land." As Billy spoke, he un-holstered his weapon and pointed it at Aradia.

"We know you don't have a phone here. You can leave here alive or live here in a grave." Falls sounded perfectly satisfied with the second option.

"Live the way you left our Lila?" There was venom in Aradia's voice.

Her accusation left Falls flummoxed for a second. Diane looked at Aradia then turned her probing gaze to Falls and gasped. Falls hoped Billy didn't notice his discomfort or the Cunningham woman's stare. Now there really was only one way out of this, as far as he was concerned.

"Billy, these demons are not going to obey God's word. Do his work and shoot them."

Billy, aiming his pistol, stopped and looked at Falls.

"You mean cut 'em down here?"

"I mean do your duty. No one will stop you."

Billy balked. Falls felt that pressure well up. His voice took on a higher tone and he began to run his words together.

"I'm ordering you, Billy – send thesebitches to theirgraves!"

"No Billy, no!" Aradia and Diane spoke in unison. Each one began to think about jumping Billy in order to save the other.

"You a mighty man ready to shoot two unarmed women, ain't you, Billy?"

They all turned to see Floyd on the porch. He stepped around in front of the women and looked Billy square in the eye.

Billy spat and grinned.

"You ain't dead yet, Floyd? You a tougher man than I thought."

"Plenty tough for you, Billy."

"I guess you are." Billy said and shot Floyd.

Dawkins and Tommy pulled up behind Falls car, which was parked behind Diane's car.

"What's Falls doin' way out here?" Dawkins was mystified.

"He and Billy might be out here looking for Floyd."

"Any idea where to start?"

Tommy was looking around when they heard a shot off to the left, in the woods. They looked at each other and took off running.

The shot hit Floyd in the chest. He didn't know why he wasn't dead. Lying on his side, he saw Billy take aim for the ladies. He pulled himself up and threw himself at

Billy in one motion. Billy, concentrating on the women, didn't even notice Floyd until he was in his line of sight.

Floyd landed hard on Billy, knocking the gun from his hand. Floyd started to rise and Billy began to rise with him. Floyd head-butted Billy, who fell back with a grunt and lay still.

'That's for the other night', Floyd thought as he stood, feeling lightheaded. He turned to face Falls, who had beaten Aradia and Diane to the gun.

"It's . . . over . . . Brother. I . . saw you . . at the . . .cabin . . ." Floyd found it hard to speak, yet very satisfying.

Falls had the look of a burning man in his eyes.

"How dare you presume to accuse me? You are devil's spawn."

Dawkins and Tommy reached the clearing to see Falls aim point blank at Floyd's stomach.

"You drop that gun, Brother!" Dawkins screamed. Falls didn't hear him. He didn't hear the angels trying to convince him otherwise. He saw Floyd's smug grin. He heard Floyd's self-satisfied voice.

"You a man of the devil, Brother. You gonna burn in hell."

Falls felt the trigger pull back, heard the sound of gunfire and saw Floyd fly back. He hardly noticed being tackled by Tommy.

Aradia and Diane ran to Floyd. Bubbles of blood were forming at the corners of his mouth.

"You're going to be all right Floyd. He saved us, sheriff – saved us both."

Floyd looked at Aradia.

"Don't . . . see . .no shadows. See . . light."

Falls had no nails left to gnaw on. They had let him have a bible, but that was all. No visitors, except his lawyer, and when he came, all he could talk about was taking the guilty plea for murder. Falls would not apologize for doing God's work. He felt the pressure all around him, all the time. He wished he could have his shoelaces. He wished he could have his belt. He wanted out. He would have settled for company, but the only company he had was that damned painting that glared down at him from the other side of the bars. The nameplate said it was some general, but Falls knew who was there on the wall to vex him.

He knew because the painting had Floyd's face, looking down on him in constant judgment. As he would until Falls could escape the pressure. He would. Sooner or later, he'd find a way. With or without God's hand.

Zeitfracht Medien GmbH
Ferdinand-Jühlke-Straße 7
99095 Erfurt, Deutschland
produktsicherheit@kolibri360.de

Druck:
CPI Druckdienstleistungen GmbH
im Auftrag der
Zeitfracht Medien GmbH
Ein Unternehmen der Zeitfracht - Gruppe
Ferdinand-Jühlke-Str. 7
99095 Erfurt